THE BAY PHANTOM

MIDNIGHT IN HELL'S CATHEDRAL

AIRSHIP 27 PRODUCTIONS

Published by Airship 27 Productions
www.airship27.com
www.airship27hangar.com

Editor: Ron Fortier
Associate Editor: Gordon Dymowski
Marketing and Promotions Manager: Michael Vance
Production and design by Rob Davis.

ISBN: 978-1-946183-81-1

Printed in the United States of America

10 9 8 7 6 5 4 3 2 1

THE BAY PHANTOM

MIDNIGHT IN HELL'S CATHEDRAL

by Chuck Miller

PROLOGUE

THE DONNER-PURDY FUNERAL HOME
FEBRUARY, 1932

"Oh, Jesus, Charlie, this dame is still alive!"

"What? That ain't possible. Look, her guts are all over the floor."

"Yeah, but—Well, they're still kind of connected, I guess. But the thing is—she's breathing."

"Breathing?"

"Yeah, and she's got a pulse. There really ain't all that much blood—Hell, she's got to be in shock. We gotta get her out of here and to a hospital right now."

"She ain't gonna make it, Len."

"She's made it this far. She's been lying here for an hour. Call an ambulance and have them bring a stretcher. Two *stretchers. We can't just dump that stuff back in her. Get some gloves, too. Jesus, her eyelids are flickering. I hope she ain't awake."*

"She can't be. And she won't be alive time we get her to a hospital, but I guess we have to try."

CHAPTER ONE
FRIENDS

AUGUST, 1932

Mirabelle Darcy climbed the pull-down ladder to the attic of Tull House, the home she shared with her friend and employer, Joe Perrone.

The house stood at the end of a lonely road on the northern edge of Mobile Bay.

The attic was the place Mirabelle had prepared to communicate with the ghosts that haunted the old place.

The "ghosts" had been quiet lately, but they were still there. Mirabelle had become sensitive to their presence, and often detected them in one room or another.

She didn't know what they really were. Maybe they were spirits, maybe they were just echoes of personalities that had existed long ago, mysteriously replaying dead thoughts and feelings, and occasionally interacting in a tentative and puzzling manner with human beings.

Mirabelle was young, just twenty-seven years of age, but she was certainly old enough not to indulge in superstition. This was not superstition.

Mirabelle sat cross-legged on the floor and lit three small candles, the flames illuminating the intense expression on her face. She felt a little foolish, but she did it solemnly, reminding herself that the ghosts, whatever they were, did exist and deserved respect.

"I know I said I wouldn't bother you again like this," she whispered, "but—I don't think it really *bothers* you, does it? I mean, you obviously crave interaction, or you wouldn't hang around. I should have promised not to give you any more instructions, like I did before. But just talking, that's okay, isn't it? Sometimes I need to talk to someone, and I don't really have anybody I can—" She shook her head.

"Well, there's Mister—I mean, there's *Joe*. He's my friend, yeah, but that's kind of new, me thinking of him that way. I've known him, on and off, for most of my life, and we're pretty close in a lot of ways. Really, he's more like family, and that's kind of the problem. Not the main part of the problem, but a significant one. What I mean is, there's always a certain distance between a person and his or her family, right?"

She was silent for a while, listening to the silence. The ghosts had nothing to say, apparently, which was not really a problem, since they seldom made any sense at all when they did speak.

"And speaking of family," she went on. "Well, that's part of my problem. See, I know some things about Joe's family that I can never tell him. He believes that his father, mother, and brother were killed by criminals when he was a kid. That's why he decided to become the Bay Phantom. And it's the truth, except for the brother part. His brother Anthony wasn't killed at all. He killed one of the men that broke into the Perrones' house that night and set a fire that burned the body beyond recognition.

"Anthony Perrone had some things wrong with him. His mind, I mean. He's brilliant, a genius, probably as smart as I am, but he... He doesn't have any moral compass at all. He's what they call a sociopath, I think.

"Anyhow, for most of his life he's been doing experiments on people. On himself too, for that matter. He did something to Joe when Joe was very young, something that gave Joe certain abilities. It made him stronger, gave him increased stamina, that kind of thing. He heals very quickly too. But a problem arose a few months ago. Joe started to become irrational. I won't go into a lot of detail now, but I figured out what had been done to him back when he was a boy, and what it was doing to him as an adult. Whatever Anthony had done to him had gone wrong, and had to be—*repaired.*

"So I had to get Anthony and bring him here, to fix what he'd done. And that was a problem, because Anthony was and is in Leavenworth Federal Prison. You know a little bit about that, but since I'm talking more for my own benefit than yours, I'll go ahead and say that I went to Leavenworth and broke Anthony Perrone out. Of course, they don't know him as Anthony Perrone there. Nobody knows him as Anthony Perrone. To the world at large, he is Doctor Piranha, the criminal mastermind who almost destroyed the city of Mobile before he was apprehended by the Bay Phantom.

"And that's my problem when it comes to Joe. I am the only person in the world who knows that Doctor Piranha is the Bay Phantom's big brother. I can never tell Joe that, not ever. I should, he deserves to know the truth, but it would kill him. It would flat-out kill him. So I have to keep this secret.

"Anthony fixed what was wrong with Joe, and let himself be captured and taken back to prison. For some reason, he wants to be there. So that worked out okay. Joe is doing better. He has no idea what I did, and he doesn't remember much of what happened when he was... sick. I've kept the truth from him, and I intend to continue doing so, and I feel terrible about it."

She had not been expecting any response. The ghosts had been silent for months. She had just wanted to vent to someone, even if that someone was not there.

She was surprised, therefore, when a sound arose in the attic, like hundreds of voices, all whispering the same thing:

Miss Mirabelle Miss Mirabelle how are you we love to hear from you we have been quiet because we thought you wanted us to it is good to hear your voice, good good good

"Uh—hello. It's good to hear you too. Are you—are you all okay?"

Blind, said the voices.

"What?" said Mirabelle. "What's wrong? You can't see?"

No no Miss Mirabelle not us we can see it is chance that is blind pure and blind

"I don't understand."

You will understand after it is too late not late enough for some you will understand no chance Miss Mirabelle there is no chance no chance

The voices faded then, until the attic was quiet, but for the sound of Mirabelle's breathing.

"Hello?" she said. "Are you there?"

Silence.

Joe Perrone sat in a chair behind a large, old desk in his office in one of the subterranean rooms beneath Tull House. He was a young man of twenty-seven, with a long face and deep-set eyes. Facing him across the desk were the black mask, goggles, and slouch hat of the Bay Phantom, currently gracing the featureless head of an old dressmaker's dummy that had belonged to Perrone's mother, several lifetimes ago.

Perrone stared at the thing for a while, then cleared his throat and spoke:

"Doctor Freud impressed upon me the importance of talking out one's problems. Unfortunately, there are very few people I can talk to openly. Actually, there are none—apart from you." He smiled ruefully. "And what on earth does that say about me?" He shook his head. "Well, no matter. Here we are. If nothing else, you are a good listener."

"There is someone I should be able to talk to more openly—Mirabelle.

She's the closest thing I have to family, but there are certain...*barriers* between us. I don't really understand what they are. Much of it has had to do with our races. She is black, and I'm white, of course. She has told me more than once that I can't possibly understand what it means to be black in the society we live in, and she's correct, I can't. I would if I could, and I must confess that it angers me to have something like that standing between me and Mirabelle. It has gotten better; the racial divide is not the hobgoblin it once was for her, but still..."

He stood up and began pacing back and forth behind the desk.

"And then there's the matter of her father. She thinks he is dead. He is not. His mind was damaged during his many years of captivity by Hector Sams. I rescued him from that and placed him in a clinic. He was showing some signs of improvement when... something happened. Another patient at the clinic, a man I know only as the Black Embalmer, escaped, and he took Paul Darcy with him. To be fair, a group of criminals had attacked the clinic with the aim of kidnapping Paul, and the Embalmer may have saved him from a rather unpleasant fate.

"The Embalmer is an... interesting character. He operates according to his own personal code. He is a criminal. He once worked as an enforcer for a band of gangsters. His particular method of dealing with rivals and dissidents was to, ah, embalm them alive. I captured him and placed him in the clinic, where a strange sort of rapport developed between us. Morally, he is a bit questionable, but... there's something about him that I find almost admirable, and I am certain that he won't harm Paul Darcy. He might even help him. I believe that and I don't know why. It might seem that I am running an awful risk by not tracking the two of them down. But I doubt that even I could find the Embalmer if he does not wish to be found.

"While I would not *trust* him in the general sense of the word, I have a certain strange faith in him, I suppose.

"But, as far as Mirabelle is concerned—I can't tell her about it, not yet. Perhaps I'm being childish, but I feel that, if I cannot come to her with unequivocally good news about her father, tell her that he is fully restored in mind, then I cannot tell her anything at all. And the fact that I have wagered Paul Darcy's future on such an, ah, unstable character as the Embalmer—Well, you see my dilemma. How can I explain to her the unfathomable faith I have in him when I can't even explain it to myself?"

He sat down again and drummed his fingers on the desk for a minute or so.

"And there are other things. Recent questions that have not been adequately answered. I'm talking about Roy Markham."

In order to infiltrate a criminal gang, the Bay Phantom had recently taken on the identity of Roy Markham, a fictional criminal persona he had used before. But this time, it had been different. The "Roy Markham" persona had almost completely taken over. Mirabelle had attributed this to the effects of Anthony Perrone's experiments, but other information had recently come to light. There really had been a man named Roy Markham, and he had once owned Tull House. Perrone knew nothing of the Anthony Perrone business, of course, and was left with nothing but questions about Markham.

"I had a dream about Roy Markham," Perrone said. "I was with him here in this house. He was sitting at this desk, and I was standing where you are. He said there was danger ahead; that a cloud was rising. A cloud like an evil umbrella, he said, dark and hot. I asked him what he meant, but he would not elaborate.

"When I woke up, I was in the library, sitting at my desk there. I have never been prone to sleepwalking, but that is what I seem to have done. I had apparently taken out a deck of Tarot cards—a gift, Charles Fort sent them to me years ago—and selected several of them, arranged them in small stacks on my desk.

"In the first stack, to my left, were the Magician, the High Priestess, the Hanged Man, and the Lovers.

"The second stack, in the middle, consisted of the Fool and the Hierophant.

"And, in the third stack, to my right, were the Tower, the Devil, Judgement, and Death.

"I cannot imagine why I would have done such a thing. If there is a psychological reason, if I was attempting some form of communication with my waking mind, it is beyond my conscious understanding."

He leaned back and stared at the ceiling for a while. Then he lowered his gaze to the dummy and smiled ruefully.

"You really don't have much to offer, do you?" he said, shaking his head. "Though I'm sure you're sympathetic, you're a poor substitute for flesh and blood. I may just have to find someone more animated to confide in."

CHAPTER TWO

A BAD WAY TO GO

"This is bad," said Detective Lieutenant Carl Matranga, feeling more than a little out of his depth. "I mean, I've seen some stuff, but this—This is *bad*."

Matranga was two years away from forty, but still in good shape. He worked hard to keep the fat off of his midsection, and there was no gray at all in his auburn hair, and his hairline had not receded more than a fraction of an inch since high school.

He was standing in an alley behind the Woolworth's store on Dauphin Street in downtown Mobile, with six uniformed cops and one plainclothes detective. The cops guarded the perimeter of the crime scene, their faces turned away from the centerpiece, a pair of corpses propped up against the whitewashed wall.

The worst part of it was that this was not the first, and Matranga had no reason to hope that it would be the last.

He had seen corpses before, too many of them, but never before in his career had he seen anything like the gruesome displays that had presented themselves recently. In this case, the man and woman had been thoroughly done in—throats cut, stomachs sliced open, guts pulled out and arranged neatly on the ground around the bodies. It looked like someone had used the gory material to make some kind of a symbol: a half circle on the pavement, terminating at the wall on either side of the bodies, with a pair of parallel lines beneath the arc.

On the wall above the bodies, something had been written in what certainly appeared to be blood. The lab boys would have to confirm it, like they had the last time. The inscription, identical to the last one, was puzzling. The writing was sloppy and not easy to make out, but it appeared to say:

$E = MC^2$

"I'm with you, Carl," said the plainclothes detectives, a fresh-faced youngster named Hunt. "This makes me think of that guy in England, whaddayacallim, Jack the Ripper."

Matranga sighed. "I wish Tom Dart was here," he said.

Hunt looked around. "Don't be wishing that too loud," he whispered. "There's ears everywhere. Tom Dart ain't to be mentioned by anybody on the force, unless they're cursing the day he was born. If the Chief gets wind of you—"

"I know, I know. But, dammit, I ain't convinced Tom's guilty."

"I'd keep that opinion to myself, if I was you. Like I say, if Chief Prater hears—"

"Yeah, yeah. Well, it don't make any difference what I think, anyhow."

"That's right. What's done is done. We're lucky we ain't in it. We've got enough to worry about with this here."

That was the truth. It was the second such double homicide in the past two weeks, and Matranga was no closer to solving the first one than he was to solving this brand-new one. He had only been a Detective Lieutenant for a short while—just since Dart got busted—and things weren't looking good for him. He needed a break, not another unsolved murder.

One of the uniformed officers approached him.

"There's a dame out on the street asking for you, Lieutenant."

Matranga made his way out of the secured area and around the corner of a building onto Conception Street.

Waiting for him was a trim blonde in a light overcoat and hat. She was scowling at a uniformed officer who looked like he wanted to be holding her by the arm, but didn't dare to. Matranga smiled. It was a genuine smile, because he always enjoyed seeing her, even though the current circumstances were not at all conducive to friendly discourse.

"Miss Turnbull," he said. "What are you doing here?"

Gladys Turnbull was an editor at the *Mobile Press*, but she couldn't break herself of the habit of going out to cover stories herself. She was a reporter at heart, not really suited to life behind a desk, and Matranga often wondered how long it would be before she voluntarily demoted herself.

"I heard something was up," she said, "and I came down here to see about it, that's what. So, what is it?"

She took a notebook from her purse and flipped it open. She fixed Matranga with a friendly, hopeful look and stood with a little pencil poised over the paper.

"Something I can't talk about," Matranga said.

"Can't or won't?"

"Same difference."

"Well—Can I have a look at what's back there?"

"Jesus, Miss Turnbull, of course not. Can't you see we got the whole area secured?"

"I'm the press, Matranga. You know, First Amendment and all that. Come on, give."

"Sorry, no can do. Not now."

She scowled at him as she closed her notebook and stuck the pencil through the spiral binding wire, and said, "You used to play fair, Matranga."

She shoved the notebook into her purse, and the little pencil went flying.

This was by design, of course. She lunged for the bouncing pencil, pretended to stumble, then ran headlong around the corner. She got to within fifteen feet of the crime scene, more than close enough to get one hell of an eyeful, before two of the uniformed cops grabbed her, turned her around, and marched her back to Lieutenant Matranga.

Gladys was looking more than a little green around the gills.

"It's okay, boys," Matranga said. "I'll talk to her. You just go keep that scene secure."

As his subordinates complied, Matranga turned to Gladys.

"Well," he said, "are you satisfied now?"

Gladys swallowed several times until she was certain she wasn't going to vomit.

"Jesus Christ, Matranga, what's going on?"

"I don't know, Miss Turnbull. I wish you hadn't seen that. I can't give you orders, but I'm asking you not to write about this, at least not right now."

She shook her head. "What would I write? All I have is what I saw, and—" She shook her head again. "What the hell happened? What do you know?"

"I can't tell you that. I can't tell you anything, honest to God. I just can't. There's a lid on this, and if it blows off, I'm gonna be in serious hot water. I can't give you orders, you're the press and all, but I'd really, really appreciate it if you'd keep this quiet, just for now. I don't suppose it can stay hushed forever. You play ball with me, and I promise you you'll get an exclusive when the time comes."

So. There was a lid on something, eh? That could very well mean that this wasn't the first such incident.

"Okay," she said, not exploring her hunch. "You've always played straight with me, Matranga, back when we were both lower on our respective ladders."

"That's right. And I'd like to keep it that way."

Gladys lowered her voice to a whisper. "Well, as long as I've got you here, what about Tom Dart?"

Matranga swallowed hard and looked around.

"I cannot talk about that," he said, his voice suddenly husky. "I just can't. If I could—Well, I can't."

"Not even all the way off the record?"

"Not even then. I'm sorry, Miss Turnbull."

This was strange. Matranga had always been open with her. He had always seemed like a rather simple man, not to say a dullard. Of course, now that he had new responsibilities, his change of attitude toward the press might be understandable. However, Gladys had the impression that his attitude hadn't changed. Something else had, something external. Matranga was under pressure.

"Okay," she said. "Like I say, you've always been straight with me, and I trust you. I know you wouldn't try to shut me out unless you had a damn good reason." Gladys was not above applying a little subtle emotional pressure herself. And it was working, she thought, based on the expression of regret and discomfort that had stolen over the man's face. Whatever was going on, it went against the man's grain. Gladys wouldn't press him too hard today, but she would keep it in mind for later.

The Tom Dart thing was rotten. She could tell Matranga knew it too, as did most of her contacts on the force. Nobody wanted to talk about it. But if she handled it properly, Matranga might. He and Tom had always been close, and whatever was going on, he had to resent it. But how much did he actually know?

"Yeah," Matranga said, not meeting her eyes. "One thing, Miss Turnbull. Don't breathe a word of this to anybody else on the force. And steer clear of Chief Prater and his boys."

"I don't talk to them anyhow. Never did trust that guy."

She waited for a moment to see if he would look at her, make some sort of appeal or promise with his eyes. When, after several moments, he did not, she nodded crisply and stuck her notebook into her purse. Just before she walked away she said, "You take care, Matranga."

"You too, Miss Turnbull," he mumbled, looking down at the sidewalk. "You too."

CHAPTER THREE
DURANCE VILE

"How much longer you got, cop?"

"I don't know," said Tom Dart. "I'm not keeping track."

The former Mobile Police Department detective currently occupied a cell on Death Row in Kilby Prison, four miles south of the state capitol in Montgomery. Six weeks earlier, he had been convicted of capital murder in the death of Alvin Branch and sentenced to die in the electric chair at Kilby, a garishly-painted monstrosity called "Yellow Mama," which had been built several years earlier by a master carpenter and convicted burglar named Ed Mason.

He sat in his tiny cell staring at the solid metal door with the little grille in it. His blonde hair was disheveled, as it always was nowadays, and his face was drawn and pale. He was talking with the man in the identical cell next to his. If they raised their voices a bit, they could hear one another just fine. The new man had been brought in that morning, and they had exchanged a bit of conversation about the food, the guards, and so forth.

"How do you not keep track of how long you got left to live?" his neighbor wanted to know.

"I just don't. Anyway, how do I know how much time I've got left? How does anybody? I could have a heart attack and die tonight."

"You got heart trouble?"

"No. But the prison could catch fire and we could all burn to death."

"Always look on the bright side, huh?" the other man said with a rueful chuckle. Then his tone became serious. "You know, I hate you 'cause you're a cop, but on a personal level, you don't seem like a bad guy. How the hell did you ever end up here? You ain't said nothing about that."

"I killed a man in cold blood. That's what they said at my trial, anyhow, and the jury bought it."

"But you ain't guilty?"

"I'm not going to say that because it's too much of a cliche."

"Too much of a who?"

"Too corny. Every guy on Death Row says he didn't do it."

"Not me, pal," the other man said boldly. "I done it and I ain't sorry."

"Well, that's refreshing, anyhow."

"Sonofabitch messed with my daughter, and I wasn't having it."

"Really? I'm a little surprised they convicted you for capital murder on a thing like that."

"You ain't never seen me, have you? You didn't see me when they brung me in today?"

"No. I never laid eyes on you. What's that got to do with it?"

"You might not tell from how I talk, but I'm colored. Guy I killed was white. Do I need to explain it any more than that?"

"No. No, you don't. What's your name?"

"I'm called Lucas Horne. I know who you are, Tom Dart, 'cause everybody's been talking about you."

"I bet. Well, it's nice to meet you, Lucas Horne. I got seventeen days left."

"Shit, man. I got four weeks. Unless, like you say, we get lucky and get heart attacks or this damn place burns down."

"Well, you never know what's gonna happen."

"My mama used to say that. She was right, too. Thing is, the shit that happens is usually bad."

The two men fell silent then, and just sat on their bunks, feeling time rushing through them like a gale.

CHAPTER FOUR
THEORIES

"I'm going to have to get him out of there," Perrone said, "and I simply do not have time to do it legally. All appeals are exhausted, no new evidence has emerged. Tom will go to the electric chair in sixteen days. I'll just have to resort to... other means, then sort out the law later on. I *have* to do it, Mirabelle."

"I'm not saying you don't," she replied. "Well, actually, yes I am. *We* have to do it, Joe, not just *you*."

Tom Dart had been accused of murdering his old mentor, Senior Detective Alvin Branch of the Mobile Police Department.

Branch had died under rather unusual circumstances during the ghastly affair of the Cannibal Guild. He had in fact been shot by a member of the International Criminal Police Commission known only as Mohammed.

Branch had been a dirty cop, in the pockets of the mysterious cabal that controlled the city of Mobile. The man called Mohammed had killed Branch as he was about to murder Tom Dart.

Those were the facts.

But when Dart had resisted the cabal that had promoted him in hopes of securing his cooperation, those facts had rapidly changed. "New evidence" had been "discovered," including a pair of "eyewitnesses." Practically everything to do with the case against Tom Dart belonged in quotation marks, but his arrest, trial, and conviction had proceeded rapidly and implacably to a conclusion which had obviously been determined before any charges were even filed.

Tom Dart's murder trial had proceeded with suspicious swiftness. District Attorney Cumber had demanded the death penalty. Tom had been found guilty and sentenced according to Cumber's demand.

What nobody in the city government knew, however, was that Tom Dart was a friend of the Bay Phantom. Not that it had done Tom much good. Joe Perrone had hired lawyers and the Bay Phantom had undertaken other means to keep Tom out of prison. None of it had worked. The frame was too perfect. The corrupt system had decided that Tom Dart was to die, and it looked like that was going to happen—and soon.

"Of course, Mirabelle," Perrone said. "You know you're included in all such operations. I get a bit careless with my pronouns now and then."

"Uh-huh. Well, I've an idea I'm working on, and I'll have something for *us* to implement soon. I'll let you know in a couple of days."

"Very good, very good. Uh, Mirabelle, something has been on my mind, and I'd like to get your opinion. We haven't really discussed it, and I'm wondering about whatever thoughts you might have."

"Sure. What is it?"

"Do you think I was actually possessed by the spirit of this Roy Markham?"

"I don't know, Joe. I suppose it's possible."

"Well—It would provide an explanation for some of my rather, er, aberrant behavior."

Yes, Mirabelle thought, *a very* convenient *explanation. I should be grateful to have it.* The truth was something she could never reveal to her friend: That his "rather, er, aberrant behavior" was not the result of a ghostly possession; that it was, in fact, the result of a series of scientific experiments conducted by Perrone's brother Anthony—better known as the diabolical super-criminal Doctor Piranha.

As far as Joe Perrone was concerned, his brother had died, along with his parents, in the incident that had sown the seeds for the eventual emergence of the Bay Phantom.

"Uh-huh," Mirabelle said. "Well, as you know, psychic research isn't really my thing. I just have to fall back on the old 'more things in heaven and earth' when it comes to that stuff."

"But it's possible."

"I said I supposed it was. That's the best I can do."

"It's very curious."

"That it is," she agreed.

In fact, she *did* wonder about it. After all, the name must have come from *somewhere.* Had Perrone read it somewhere at some point and subconsciously used it when they were constructing his criminal identity? Or was there something more metaphysical at work?

"I need to talk with someone," Perrone said.

"I'm someone," Mirabelle replied. "You're talking with me."

"No, I mean someone with some—ah, spiritual authority."

"Oh, for God's sake."

"Precisely that. I may be a lapsed Catholic, but I'm still a Catholic. And I cannot remember the last time I went to Confession."

"In your case, that's a good thing, don't you think? I mean, you start confessing stuff, and you're liable to wind up in the hot seat along with Tom Dart."

"Mirabelle, I know you're not a believer, but you have certainly heard of the Seal of the Confessional."

"Oh, hell, is *that* what you're planning on doing? Seriously? If this is about that Markham thing—"

Perrone shook his head. "No, it isn't just that. In fact, it isn't that at all. It's—*everything.* Everything that I've been doing."

"It seems like a bad idea to me."

"When I was a child," he said, "our priest was Father Craig. He's Archbishop now. You know that old family Bible in the front room? That was a gift from him."

"Okay."

"I'm going to give him a call. He has an office at the Cathedral, and I understand he is in town for the next little while."

"Okay."

"I think I'll feel much better if I do, Mirabelle."

"Okay."

"I'm serious."

"I said *okay*. Who are you trying to convince? Me or yourself?"

"But you don't think it's a good idea."

"You know that," Mirabelle said, exasperated. "I'm not going to change my mind, and I'm not going to keep telling you over and over. Go do what you're going to do and quit pestering me about it."

It would have been best for Joe to remain silent at this point, but he felt an irrational need to continue to pursue the topic from a slightly different angle. Fortunately for his relations with Mirabelle, just as he drew breath to speak, the telephone rang and she went to answer it.

"It's for you, Joe. Gladys."

He took the receiver from Mirabelle, who pointedly did not look at him, and spoke:

"Hello, Gladys, how are you?"

Gladys Turnbull had discovered the Bay Phantom's identity during an earlier bout of investigative reporting, was one of his trusted friends and confidantes. She had elected to keep his secret to herself, and to aid the Phantom in his activities.

"Hi, Joe. Well, I'm doing better than some people, considering the fact that my guts are still inside my body."

"Come again?"

She told him of the peculiar murders and Matranga's peculiar attitude toward them. She also told him of her own rather clumsy effort to gather information.

"I didn't get a real good look," she said, "but there were two people, it looked like they had been gutted, and it looked like they'd been—*posed*. Also, there was an inscription on the wall over the bodies. I think it was written in blood."

"Very dramatic. Were you able to read it?"

"I think so. I only saw it for a second, but it looked to me like it said $E=MC^2$."

"Really? That's interesting."

"It certainly is. I wonder if these dumb cops know the significance of that formula."

"Can you remember any details of how the bodies were, ah, arranged?"

"I didn't get that good a look. But, here's the thing, Joe: I got the strong impression that this isn't the first time something like this has happened recently."

"I see. Well, try to find out whatever else you can. Without putting yourself into too much jeopardy, of course."

"I'll do my best, but I can't say I'm very hopeful. Something is going on downtown. Matranga is a good man, but he's under some heavy pressure, I think. Chief Prater and the rest of the gang at city hall. They're trying to cover these killings up, that's the impression I got. I'm not surprised that they're corrupt, but what is their interest in a series of gruesome murders? That takes corruption to a whole new level."

"Indeed," Perrone said. "Well, you be careful, and let me know when you find out anything more." He hung up.

"So, what are you going to do?" Mirabelle asked him, after he had recounted the information given to him by Gladys.

"The only thing for it is a patrol. I'll go out myself, and of course I'll have Shorty and Louis keep their eyes open.

"And I have another idea, Mirabelle. Half the police department is owned by the cabal who were involved with the Cannibal Guild. But who owns, or at least has a long-term lease on the other half?"

"Well, that would be—Oh, no. Joe, I don't think you ought to—"

"There's nothing else for it, Mirabelle." He sighed sharply. "I'm going to have to pay a visit to Penny Carter."

"No," Mirabelle said. "I'll go. She knows who I am, she knows who you are, she knows who everyone is. I met her while you were sick, and we have a sort of relationship. She's too smart for you, but not for me. I can keep my head. It just makes sense."

"All right then. I can't find any fault with anything you say."

At least, Mirabelle reflected, he had sense enough to know she was right. Perrone had a history with Penny Carter. He was fascinated with her, nursing an unhealthy infatuation. Penny had the ability to wind him around her little finger. But Mirabelle Darcy was nowhere near as malleable.

CHAPTER FIVE
MISTER NESS

Treasury Agent Eliot Ness had sort of figured that the remainder of his career as a lawman, after the fall of Al Capone (for which, to his mind, he had received insufficient credit), would take something of a downhill trajectory. He just hadn't expected it to be quite so precipitous.

In April, Ness and some of his "Untouchables" had escorted Capone from his cell in the Cook County Jail in Chicago to the Dearborn Street train station, where the gangster would board an express bound for Atlanta, and the federal penitentiary there, where he would spend the next eleven years. It had been the climax of many long and arduous months, and once it was over, Ness had felt washed-out and depressed. Ness would continue his work as a Prohibition agent, but the Big Game had been won, it was over, and there were no more championships on the horizon. Everyone seemed to agree, moreover, that Prohibition itself was on the way out, and might be repealed within the next year or two.

And now here Ness was, in Mobile, Alabama, of all places. Was he here to bust some untouchable crime boss? To break up a bootlegging ring?

No.

He was here to find a goddamn werewolf.

That was the story, anyhow. There was more to it than that—a *lot* more. But the Werewolf was to be his entree to the police department. There was something funny going on in Mobile, Alabama, and Ness's superiors wanted him to find out just what it was. The city government was thoroughly corrupt. This had been demonstrated several times recently. The affair of the International Patriots Guild, which had, as the name suggested, international complications, had been settled after a fashion, but not to the complete satisfaction of the federal government. Minor reforms had been made, but nothing had really changed.

J. Edgar Hoover, director of the Justice Department's Bureau of Investigation, had personally asked Ness to undertake this little fact-finding expedition. It didn't hurt that there was a deep connection to Ness' earlier activities against the Capone organization in Chicago.

Eliot Ness had a knack for finding small threads that could unravel large conspiracies. He had that going for him. It seemed to be an integral part of his mental and emotional makeup.

He got off the train at the terminal in downtown Mobile. It was his first trip to the Deep South, and he wondered if he would get acclimated to the summer heat and humidity. It felt like a goddamn sauna down here, with a hot breeze blowing in off of Mobile Bay, bringing with it an unpleasant fishy odor. He fetched his luggage from a porter, a Negro more servile

He was here to find a goddamn werewolf.

and downtrodden than any he had ever encountered in the North—but, admittedly, not by much—and took a cab to the Battle House Hotel. Once he got his belongings squared away, which took about five minutes, he picked up the phone and had the hotel switchboard operator connect him with Mobile police headquarters.

"I need to talk to a Lieutenant Carl Matranga," he told the bored-sounding character who answered the call. He was asked to identify himself, and he did so. He was told to wait, and he did that too, for almost ten minutes.

He was told that Lieutenant Matranga was not available, but would he care to leave a message?

"No, I'll get in touch with him later," Ness said testily, before slamming down the phone.

He rented a car from a small agency and drove out to the federal hospital where Gerald Sams, aka the Werewolf, had been held for several weeks before his mysterious disappearance.

The director of the hospital repeated for Ness the same short story he had told countless other law officers and federal agents: The Werewolf had been kidnapped from the facility by a group of masked, armed men. Ness pressed him for small details about the men's clothing, the exact words they had used, and so forth. He provided nothing of any value. He was holding something back, Ness was sure. The man was scared of something or somebody. If Ness had actually given a damn about the Werewolf, he would have pressed the man until he squealed, but he gave it just enough to make it look good. Ness had been loud and aggressive, and made sure several other employees overheard him. He had a feeling the word would get around.

He finally managed to get Matranga on the phone and arrange a meeting, though the Lieutenant didn't seem remotely enthusiastic about it. Well, that was understandable. Though Ness was something of a celebrity, Matranga didn't know him from Adam on any kind of personal or professional level. If Ness' speculations regarding the lieutenant were accurate, the man would be suspicious of anyone who approached him the way Ness was doing. It wouldn't be easy for Ness to sell himself to the man.

They met in Matranga's office. The lieutenant was friendly enough, and pledged his cooperation in the search for the Werewolf, though he didn't think there was much he could do. Ness asked him a few of the questions he had prepared, and gotten the answers he had expected: none. It was when he steered his inquiries to other matters, like the recent affair of the International Patriots Guild—in which the Werewolf had had some reported involvement—that Matranga began to get vague. The man seemed downright nervous when Ness brought up anything to do with city government, and he began to squirm uncomfortably when the subject of Tom Dart came up. Ness didn't know for sure that the young detective's murder conviction had any connection to the things he was interested in, but he had developed a hunch, and it seemed, judging by Matranga's reaction, that he had been right. He didn't think Matranga knew any specifics, but it was plain to see that he thought the whole business was rotten.

Ness also met with the mayor and the Chief of Police. They were frosty toward him, though outwardly polite. They made a fuss over the celebrity federal agent and congratulated him on the downfall of Al Capone, and that was about all he could hope to get out of them.

Matranga was the key, Ness was certain. He would just have to drag out his bogus Werewolf investigation as long as he could, and continue working on the man.

CHAPTER SIX

RICKEY AT THE RESCUE MISSION

This is a hell of a way to end up at nineteen years old, thought Rickey Harvard. Here he was, in the prime of life, standing in a line with a bunch of bums at the St. Dymphna Rescue Mission.

He'd had an awful couple of years. He had been tormented by ghosts and by his father and had been unable to keep a job. After he had been nearly killed and eaten by some kind of a mad scientist down underneath Dauphin Street at Mardi Gras, he had run out of money and his old man had thrown him out of the house.

He wouldn't starve, thanks to St. Dymphna's, but the soup they gave out wasn't very good, and you had to listen to a bunch of preaching to even get that much.

On this night, Rickey sat through the sermon and was sitting at one of the long tables, sipping his soup, next to an acquaintance of his, Gus Kerr. Gus was a long-time vagabond who had not held a job since Grover Cleveland was president. He was thin and dry as an Egyptian mummy, with a large, lightbulb-shaped head that looked like someone had blindly glued a few wisps of dirty cotton on it.

After the sermon was over—something about a king who had killed some people then felt bad about it—the man who kept watch over the front door got up at the podium to make an announcement:

"We're looking for volunteers to attend our special prayer group. Anybody who is selected will receive twenty dollars. Any interested parties please see me at the rear of the hall in ten minutes."

"Twenty bucks!" Rickey exclaimed, turning to Gus. "That sounds good, don't it? Maybe we should volunteer for that."

"I ain't never heard of nobody having to volunteer for a prayer group," Gus said skeptically. "And what's so special about it?"

"Aw, who knows with these religious guys? You probably gotta go out in public and talk to strangers about Jesus or something. I don't mind doing that for twenty bucks."

"I dunno, Rickey. I don't trust these guys. I mean, the soup's good and all, but there's something not quite right about this whole operation."

"What do you mean?"

"I been around a long time. This mission's been here a while too, but I ain't never seen such goings-on as I've seen in the last six months. There's gangsters and weirdos coming in and out, and there's somebody called Kraken I've heard talked about. I think I seen him once, out around the back. All dressed up in a purple robe, with a funny hat on his head."

"Aw, religious people are like that," Rickey said dismissively. "They like to dress up and act mysterious. And, as far as them gangsters go, these church people are probably trying to save their souls or something. Anyhow, that twenty bucks is for me!"

"I wouldn't fool with it, kid. Men come in here and volunteer for that group and nobody ever sees 'em again."

"Well, they probably get their soul saved and get jobs, or whatever people do. That's how come you don't see 'em no more."

Rickey thought for a while, or tried to, but he didn't have much to work with, and the thin soup didn't provide much energy to his brain. So he just made a decision without going through a whole lot of deliberation.

"I'm gonna volunteer, Gus. Think of the meal I could get with twenty bucks!" He licked his lips like a hungry cat in a cartoon he'd seen, back when he could afford to go to the show.

"Suit yourself, Rickey. Me, I'll just stick with what I know."

"Nobody ever got nowhere in this world thinking like that," Rickey declared. He got up and moved to the rear of the hall with half a dozen other hopeless hopefuls.

"Beat it, kid," said the man when he got to Rickey. "You're too young. We ain't got no use for you."

"What? Why not?"

"We're looking to save souls, kid. We need guys with plenty of sins under their belts. You look like you're about thirteen years old. You ain't had time to do nothing to be saved from."

"Like hell!" Rickey exclaimed. "I'm nearly twenty, and I've sinned plenty! I've stole stuff, and been a drunkard, and looked at dirty pictures, and I don't know what all."

The man pinned Rickey with a menacing glare, pointed to the front of the hall, and said, "You can walk the hell out of here now, as you are, or you can do it with two black eyes. I leave it up to you."

Rickey gritted his teeth. He thought about giving the guy some more lip, but he didn't think it would help his cause, and he was pretty sure the guy was serious about the black eyes. So he gave the man one last look, the nastiest one he could muster, and stomped off toward the exit.

Hell with this salvation business anyhow, he thought as he stood out in front of the whitewashed building that housed the mission. *Buncha crap is all it is. They're probably running some kind of racket in there.* His father had always told him to be careful around these religious types. Maybe the old man had been right for once.

After a while, Rickey drifted around the side of the building, to a spot near the back fence where three or four guys could always be found, telling improbable stories and sharing bottles of cheap wine. He sidled up to them and stood there, accepting the bottle and taking a sip whenever it came around to him. The stuff tasted like turpentine, but it was better than nothing.

The men were discussing a variety of topics that meant nothing to Rickey. He remained silent, just waiting for the wine bottle to reach him again. He noticed that there was a white van parked close to the back door of the mission. That was funny. He'd never seen that around here before. It was a big, boxy Ford, and it reminded Rickey of the paddy wagons used by the police.

After fifteen minutes or so, the nasty doorman who had so rudely rejected Rickey stepped out of the rear door of the building, followed by a gaggle of seven rummies.

"All right," he said loudly, "we got our candidates for tonight."

Two men got out of the van. A tall guy and a short guy. A pair of crooks for sure, Rickey figured. He knew the type. Something was wrong here.

The two crooks herded all the rummies into the back of the van, then got back into the cab. The engine started, and the vehicle drove around the side of the building and out onto Water Street.

"Well," said one of the men in the wine-sharing group, "that's the last we'll ever see of them guys."

Rickey shuddered. Suddenly, he was glad he'd been rejected for whatever it was those guys were doing.

CHAPTER SEVEN

MURDERS

Mirabelle's efforts to find and speak with Penny Carter had come to nothing. Nobody knew where she was. There were plenty of rumors. She had gone to Europe, to South America, to New York City. Mirabelle would not have been surprised to hear that she was on the moon.

There was a persistent rumor in the underworld—several members of which were related to Mirabelle by blood or marriage—that Penny had been squeezed out for good by some unknown party, and had elected to cut her losses and leave town with whatever assets she had left.

Mirabelle wasn't sure whether to believe it or not.

The Bay Phantom's irregular nighttime patrols paid off on Tuesday night. Since there was no discernible geographical pattern to the killings, there was no real pattern to his patrol route. The odds of his chancing upon a murder were astronomical, according to Mirabelle. She had told him that she wouldn't even bother trying to make the calculations. It would be pure, blind chance if he were to stumble upon another killing, she had said.

And he had agreed. But he had no leads, practically no information at all, and no other way to proceed.

He hadn't believed that it would work, and he hadn't believed that it would not. He had gone out with a simple faith that something *might* happen. And *something* turned that remote probability into an actuality.

He found them at eleven o'clock, on Durant Street, a short, dead-end cul-de-sac, half a block long, with houses on both sides and a barn-like structure at the end. He almost passed it by, but thought he caught some movement out of the corner of his eye. He stopped his car, backed up a bit, and turned right, proceeding down the little street.

There were two of them, a pair of men, and they had two bodies propped up against the side of the building at the end of the street. Those two poor people were obviously dead, their torsos ripped wide open. The men were busy arranging something on the ground around them. When the headlights of the Phantom's automobile illuminated their grisly work, the men straightened up and turned.

The Bay Phantom braked to a stop fifteen feet from the men and slipped out of the car.

"This is absolutely disgraceful," he said sternly. "What sort of explanation do you men have for this butchery?"

The Phantom got a good look at both of them. One was very tall, the other very short. The tall one put the Phantom in mind of an animated cadaver, while the short one looked as though he might belong to some species of malevolent ape. They wore dark suits and long, light blue gloves that appeared to be made of rubber, and were smeared and dripping with blood and bits of gore. The Phantom swallowed hard. He had left his headlights on, and the men's shadows swelled and crawled up the wall of the building behind them as the moved a bit closer to him. Between the two shadows, the Phantom read the message written in smeared red characters:

$E=MC^2$

"You might as well give yourselves up," the Phantom said. "You both obviously need psychiatric help. An insanity plea might not be out of the question."

The tall man uttered an obscene insult and drew a revolver from inside his jacket. The small man did the same. They said nothing, merely took aim at the Phantom and opened fire.

The Phantom seemed to shimmer and flow, first to one side, then the other, easily evading the shots. He drew his own automatic, but he was determined to take these two alive, to be turned over to the police.

He fired a shot that just grazed the sleeve of the tall man, and another that took a nip out of the short one's hat.

"You fellows would be well advised to give up at this point," he told them. "You may not feel inclined to, but I assure you that my bullets can come a lot closer if you make it necessary."

The two men fired again, with the same result as before. The Phantom was still not ready to return fire, not until he had exhausted every other option. There was always the chance he might kill them without intending to, and it would be much better to take them alive, to find out just what was going on.

The gunfire had brought several nearby residents out onto their porches and, in a couple of cases, into the street.

"Get back inside, you people!" the Phantom shouted. "Someone call the police!"

An elderly lady shouted back that she already had, and she didn't appreciate a bunch of punks yelling and shooting off firecrackers in the middle of the night.

"Ma'am," the Phantom said, not taking his eyes from the two killers, "You should go back inside. I have this under control."

"Are you sure about that?" the tall man asked with a sneer.

"Honestly," the Phantom said to them, "though there are two of you and only one of me, you're still outnumbered." He moved a bit closer, drawing a second automatic and covering both of them.

The two men looked at one another, then back at the Phantom.

"You think we're outnumbered, huh? Show him how outnumbered we are, Mouse."

The short one stuck two fingers into his mouth and gave a loud whistle.

Immediately, the street was filled with shabby, shambling figures, men made of sticks and straw, draped pale skin. Their eyes were vacant. They came from between the houses and from behind the little building that had been made the scene of the atrocity.

"Oh dear," said the Phantom.

The men surged toward him. He saw absolutely nothing in their eyes, no intelligence, no reason. They were like mechanical things. Two of them held long-bladed knives. The Phantom concentrated on them, easily disarming them. None of these poor creatures posed any real threat, but their sheer numbers, coupled with the Phantom's desire to spare them any serious harm, made them a vexing problem.

One of the men managed to get his hands on the Phantom's mask. Fumbling fingers pulled the blue goggles askew, momentarily blinding the masked man.

The Phantom kicked the man in the leg, misjudging the necessary force, and breaking the knee. The poor creature fell to the pavement and began crawling around, dragging himself with his hands, unable to stand up.

"I'm sorry," the Phantom, adjusting his goggles. "I didn't mean to—"

Another of the revenants jumped onto his back. The Phantom threw himself backward, thudding against a lamp post. He heard something crack, and the man's grip loosened. The Phantom was able to throw off his attacker, who lay in the grass, squirming, obviously gravely injured, but showing no sign of pain on his masklike face.

"Call the police," the Phantom reiterated to the bewildered and pajamaed citizens, "and for the love of God, stay indoors!"

The Phantom noticed something then that had failed to command his conscious attention earlier. The air above his head was filled with small globes of light, like large fireflies. He realized that they had been present the entire time he'd been here. He peered at them and saw nothing but pale yellow globes of light. There was no sign of any source, anything they might be attached to.

The men who had remained standing had started moving toward the open end of the little street, and the odd "fireflies" seemed to be following them. Perhaps something could be learned by following the queer procession. There was nothing more he could do here, and the police should arrive soon. The Phantom got back into his car and doused the headlights. At least the ghastly scene against the building would no longer be illuminated, and he hoped that any of the neighborhood residents who had not seen it would be spared.

The Phantom started the engine, backed up into a driveway, and headed out. The men crossed Durant Street in a body, then wandered off across a vacant lot. He kept pace with them by driving halfway around the block and intercepting them as they started off down another dark street.

The Phantom could hear sirens from various directions, and he imagined they were all converging on the crime scene he had just left.

The shambling men seemed to be heading toward downtown. There were perhaps fifteen of them. As they got closer to Broad Street, members of the group began to drift off, by ones and twos, into alleyways and spaces between buildings. And, for each man who broke off from the group, one of the floating globes of light vanished. The Phantom followed the main body across Broad and into the warren of streets that lay beyond.

He did not dare stop until the last man had entered an alley and the last floating light had disappeared. But the men had led him exactly nowhere. They had merely distributed themselves among seemingly random locations across an area of several blocks. The Phantom stopped his car and got out, following the final shambler into his chosen alleyway.

The man seemed to have fallen into a deep sleep on the ground. He was breathing and his pulse was strong and regular. The Phantom gingerly lifted him from the ground and carried him to the automobile, placing him in the back seat.

Then he drove north, to Prichard, a mostly-black community where Doctor Ambrose V. Atticus lived and worked.

Atticus was a cousin of Mirabelle's, a more-than-competent physician and an excellent research chemist. He had been helpful to the Phantom on more than one occasion.

He lifted the unconscious man from the back seat and went to Atticus' front door, knocking on it with the toe of his shoe.

After just a few seconds, the door opened the few inches allowed by the security chain, and Atticus, who seemed never to sleep, peered out. He was in his early sixties, though the skin on his face was smooth. He was almost completely bald, with tufts of white hair around his ears, and he regarded the Phantom through the lenses of a pair of wire-rim spectacles.

"Oh, hello, Mister Phantom," he said. "You do show up at the damnedest times."

"And with the, ah, darnedest things, yes."

"Well, whatcha got this time? Come on in." He shut the door, undid the chain, and opened it wide.

The Phantom followed Doctor Atticus down the narrow hallway to the small examining room at the rear of the house.

"I'm not entirely sure what I've got," he said as he placed the fellow gently on the examining table. "It's a man, as you can see, and I believe something has been done to him. I have no idea what."

"He looks drugged."

"That's what I suspect. I need to know what has been used on him."

Atticus nodded. "I'll do some blood work and see what I can find. He can stay here tonight. If he doesn't come around by morning, I can take him to the clinic, if you'd like."

"Yes, I'd appreciate that. I'll leave it to you, then. Please phone me at the number I gave you when you know something."

CHAPTER EIGHT
THE HORROR

"I don't think they're gonna be able to keep *this* one out of the papers," Gladys Turnbull said dryly. She had learned about the events on Durant Street and collared Lieutenant Matranga just outside the perimeter of the crime scene.

Matranga sighed and said, "No, ma'am, neither do I."

"So I can print all the details?"

"I can't stop you. Hell, a hundred people have seen it by now anyhow. Everybody that lives on this street got an eyeful of those stiffs before we carted 'em off."

"Right. Do you have any leads?"

"Two guys were arrested. They were found close to the scene, and they both had knives on them."

The police had established a wide perimeter around the crime scene, and no one was being allowed in, but they weren't trying to pretend like nothing had happened, and they were releasing a few details.

"You don't sound too happy about that," Gladys said.

Matranga shrugged. "I don't think they did it. Don't quote me on that, for God's sake. The Chief is taking the position that we've caught the killers. And, on top of that, all the witnesses say the Bay Phantom was here. They say he fought with the killers, then took a powder."

"Can I write about the others? The ones before this?"

"Might as well. I'm afraid I can't give you any details right now. The Chief's gonna release a statement later today, so you can get everything you need then, I guess."

A car pulled up to the curb close to where they were standing and stopped. A man got out, and walked around the front of the vehicle, nodding politely at Matranga.

"Oh, hello, Mister Ness," Matranga said. "Guess you heard about what happened, huh?"

"That I did," said Eliot Ness. "Thought maybe you could use a hand, as long as I'm here anyhow. Not that you can't handle it, but I—"

"Naw," Matranga said. "I don't know that I *can* handle it, and any help you can give would be welcome. Oh, this is Gladys Turnbull, she works for the local paper. Miss Turnbull, Eliot Ness."

"Well," Gladys said, shaking hands with the federal agent, "I'm impressed, Matranga. I didn't know you ran in such exalted circles! It's a pleasure to meet you, Mister Ness. You did this nation a great service when you helped put Capone away."

"Thank you, ma'am. I'd say something like 'It was all in a day's work,' but I've never been given to false modesty."

Gladys laughed. "I like that. People should be aware of their own capabilities. Well, Matranga, I'd better get back to the office if I'm gonna file this story and then make it to the press conference. Nice meeting you, Mister Ness. Maybe I can interview you while you're here."

"Maybe so, ma'am. Nice meeting you too."

Gladys left them, climbing into her roadster and taking off. She could just make the afternoon deadline if she hurried.

"Okay, Matranga," Ness said, rubbing his hands together, "what have we got?"

Matranga sighed. "You tell me."

The press conference was at noon, in front of City Hall. The steps leading up to the entrance had been roped off, and a gaggle of journalists were gathered on the sidewalk, among them Gladys Turnbull.

Gladys saw a lot of familiar faces, old friends and former colleagues. Reporters had come from papers as far away as New Orleans and Miami.

Local representation consisted of her and a spotty-faced young man from WODX radio, who looked as though he would rather be just about anyplace else but here. He had no recording or broadcasting equipment with him. Like Gladys, he appeared content with a pad and pencil.

She had a photographer with her, Clem Persons, a lanky seventy-year-old who had worked at the paper for more than three-quarters of his life.

As the sun reached its zenith in the sky, three men stepped through the front doors of City Hall and out to the front of the roped-off area: Police Chief Maxwell Prater, Mayor Gordon Armstadt, and District Attorney Benton Cumber.

The Mayor took point. He cleared his throat and squinted down at a sheet of paper he held in his hand.

"Greetings, members of the press," he said, without looking up at the members of the press. "We wish to announce that two men have been arrested in connection with the recent murders. Their names are Rex Tyler and Carter Hall, and they are being held in the city jail in lieu of bond.

"We believe that these killings have been orchestrated, for reasons unknown, by the so-called Bay Phantom, who was observed by a number of citizens at the scene of the recent outrage. He is being sought for questioning, but, owing to his legendary elusiveness, we have ordered our officers to shoot on sight—to wound, if possible. But make no mistake, this Phantom is a dangerous individual, probably mentally unbalanced, and no police officers will take unnecessary risks to apprehend him."

At this point, Chief Prater stepped forward. "We realize that the Bay Phantom is seen by some as a hero. It is the position of the Mobile Police Department that he is a vigilante. Let me make it clear that he is not being formally charged with anything in connection with these killings. We merely want to question him. The shoot-on-sight order is simply a measure to protect our brave police officers. If the Bay Phantom steps forward and deals with us peaceably, he will not be harmed. He will be afforded all the rights guaranteed to any citizen under the law."

He nodded and stepped back.

D.A. Cumber apparently had nothing to add. Gladys nudged Clem. He raised his trusty Speed Graphic and snapped a picture.

The mayor finally looked up from his sheet of paper and surveyed the assembled reporters, blinking like he had just emerged from a dark hole into the sunshine.

"No questions," he said. "Thank you."

Gladys watched the men retreat back into the building. Then she rubbed her eyes. For just a second, she thought she'd seen a couple of fireflies follow them through the doorway.

After she filed her story, and before the photo came back from the darkroom, Gladys phoned Joe Perrone and told him what had been said. He took the news with his customary equanimity. Gladys wondered if he ever actually got upset over anything other than vulgar language. He thanked her for the information and told her to take care.

As she hung up the phone, Clem entered her small, glassed-in office. He was holding a still-damp photo print by a thumb and forefinger.

"Sorry, Gladys," he said. "The photo's no good. I dunno what could have happened." He showed her the print. Most of it looked fine, everything was in focus—except for the faces of Prater, Armstadt, and Cumber. They were just blurs, as though someone had rubbed a thumb on the three faces when the print was still wet. Clem assured her this was not the case.

"I never seen anything like it," he said, scratching his head.

"Neither have I," she said, biting her lip. Something about the photo sent a chill through her. "Well, toss it, Clem, and we'll use file photos of the mayor and the others."

CHAPTER NINE

CHESTER

Mirabelle's cousin Chester worked at City Hall, as a custodian and occasional electrician. He was in an excellent position to pick up tidbits of information that could be useful to the Bay Phantom, and Mirabelle had decided some time back to put him on the payroll. Just about anything that might be going on at police headquarters eventually reached Chester's ears.

That was the thing about being a Negro in this society; in some ways, it rendered a person invisible. White people tended not to watch what they said around the black people who acted as their servants, any more than they would around a small child or a pet.

Mirabelle found it infuriating, but had to admit that it was useful in her current work.

Chester knew that Mirabelle did some work for the Bay Phantom. She had told him that, and he had been excited about the prospect. He was a smart, imaginative man, and he had been pinned down in a servile position for too many years. The idea that he was entering into a righteous conspiracy appealed to him.

She met him at Julius Pitts' Cafe, a grimy little storefront eatery. The place had been there forever, and was run now by Mrs. Julius Pitts, the eponymous Julius having passed away some time prior to the turn of the century.

Chester was in his fifties, but he looked closer to seventy. Life had not been easy for him, which didn't exactly set him apart from most black Southerners. His parents had been slaves, and then sharecroppers, and that was as far as they had ever gone in life. Chester had started out working on the farm in Chunchula, Alabama from sunup until sundown, beginning at the age of six and continuing for ten years, until he decided to move to the city to seek his fortune. All he ever found was one menial job after another, at least a dozen of them over the years.

Mirabelle joined Chester at a booth in the middle of the small, narrow dining room. He stood and kissed her on the cheek, as he always did.

The little cafe was known for excellent barbecue and indifferent fried chicken. Chester ordered the former, while Mirabelle contented herself with a glass of water.

"So, what have you got for me, Chester?" she asked. "Been hearing some interesting things, huh?"

"I hear plenty," said Chester. "You know how white folks are. They don't pay no more attention to an ol' darkie emptyin' their trash baskets than they would a cat. It must be the same way with that white fellow you work for, that Perrone."

"Oh, he pays attention to me sometimes," Mirabelle said, with the hint of a smirk. "Not nearly enough, though."

Chester nodded. "That's how they all are. I figure the Bay Phantom must be colored under that mask. Wouldn't no white man do the things he does for folks."

"I don't really know who the Bay Phantom is," Mirabelle said. "I just know I believe in what he's trying to do."

Chester nodded. "Well, as far as what I've got for you today, there's a fellow been hanging around police headquarters the last couple days. He's been askin' lots of questions about a couple of names on that list you give me. He's been asking about that Werewolf, for one, and he's also interested in the Bay Phantom. In fact, he talks a heap more about the Phantom and other things than he does the Werewolf."

"Who is this fellow, do you know?"

"Oh, I sure do, Mirabelle. Wait til you hear this! It's that Eliot Ness, from Chicago. You know, the one that fought ol' Al Capone."

Mirabelle sat back in her chair, momentarily nonplussed.

"That's interesting," she said. "Eliot Ness, huh?"

"Yep. He looks just like his pictures in the papers, too. He's shorter than I thought he'd be, though."

"People usually are. You say he was asking about the Werewolf?"

There was nothing to worry about there. Gerald Sams, aka the Werewolf, had been more or less cured of the pathological mental condition that had

"It's that Eliot Ness from Chicago."

made him a murderous monster.

Poor Gerald had been the subject of experimentation by Doctor Piranha, experimentation which had turned the normally inoffensive young man into the superhuman killing machine known as the Werewolf. Piranha, during his recent spell of liberty in Mobile, had reversed the process, restoring Gerald to normal—or as normal as could be expected, all things considered. He was currently in Vienna, being treated by Mirabelle's friend Dr. Sigmund Freud.

"Yep," Chester said. "A little bit. Way I see it, that was how he got his foot in the door, if you know what I mean. I think he's really here lookin' into the police department itself. That whole place is rotten, Mirabelle. Why, if I could find a better job—" He shook his head. "It's just rotten. Like I say, this Ness has been asking a lot about the Bay Phantom, and Tom Dart too. It was real dirty how they done that boy, just terrible. Everybody knows it too, but they're all afraid to talk."

Chester then turned his attention to his barbecue. Mirabelle sipped her water and thought. She had known Chester for a long time. There was something about him today that was off, a strange diffidence to his manner.

"Something else is bugging you, Chester," she said. "What is it?"

He looked up at her, momentarily surprised. He finished chewing his food, swallowed it, and said, "Well—Aw, it ain't nothing. Just something I dreamed about."

"Dreamed?"

He nodded. "Yeah. I dreamed about your daddy. Paul. You know, I ain't seen him since just before he passed, and that was a long time ago, but— In this dream I had, he was older, like he would be now, if he was alive. He was—He was sittin' in a room somewhere, talkin' to someone, but I couldn't see nobody else there in the dream. It was like he was talking to the air, Mirabelle. Somebody, whoever he was talkin' to, said something to him, and then he turned right to me and said, 'Chester, remind Mirabelle about the sword.' I wonder does that mean anything?"

"Of course not," she said. "I don't know anything about a—Well, it was just a dream, Chester. Dreams don't mean anything."

When she got back home she sat down in the kitchen and poured herself a glass of wine. She sipped it while she wrote out a report on Chester's observations on the situation downtown for Perrone, who was away from the house on some business of his own.

When she was done, she set the sheets of paper aside and thought about Chester's dream. Why would he dream about Paul Darcy? Dreams had meaning, but only within themselves and the mind of the dreamer; they were meaningless in the context of the waking world. So why had Chester's account disturbed her so?

The phone rang. A welcome interruption to Mirabelle's thoughts. She drained her glass of wine and picked up the receiver.

"Hello? Yes, this is Miss Darcy... She is? Yes... Yes, I will. I'll be there shortly, thank you."

CHAPTER TEN
CONFESSION

"Thank you for seeing me, Father Craig. I'm sorry, I mean *Archbishop*."

"Certainly, Joe, any time," Craig said warmly. "It's good to see you. I know you had some... difficulties after your family, ah, passed the way they did. I hoped we hadn't lost you. I must admit, I was a bit surprised when you phoned."

Perrone had arranged to meet with Craig in an office the Archbishop was using on the upper story of the Cathedral Basilica of the Immaculate Conception in downtown Mobile. The grand old Greek Revival style building was much as Perrone remembered from the last time he'd been inside, many years before, in spite of some obviously ongoing renovation work, which actually amounted more to restoration of a number of interior features, coupled with improvements to the plumbing, ductwork, and so forth. Some scaffolding was in place inside the sanctuary, and drop cloths were spread over some of the statuary.

Craig's office was spacious, but somewhat monkish in its simplicity and lack of adornment. The only thing hanging on any of the walls was a photograph of the bespectacled Holy Father, Pius XI, which occupied a frame behind the dark wooden desk.

Craig himself was much as Perrone remembered him. He seemed not to have aged at all. Though he was past sixty, he might have been in his forties.

"Yes," Perrone said, "well, I need a sort of favor, you see. I'm afraid I haven't been, well, the best churchgoer, and it has been quite some time since my last confession. I was sort of hoping you might—"

Craig smiled. "I'd be more than happy to hear your confession, Joe. I'm pleased to learn that you aren't the apostate I had feared you were. We can do it now, if you'd like."

"I don't—Should we go down to the Confessional?"

"No need to be so formal, Joseph. We can speak right here. As an Archbishop, I have a bit more latitude, you see. Just go sit on that divan over by the window. You can face away from me; we can maintain some of the traditions of the Confessional."

Perrone settled himself on the divan and half-closed his eyes.

"Bless me, Your Grace," he said, "for I have sinned."

"You can just call me *Father*, Joe. We're old friends, after all. I want you to feel comfortable with me."

"Yes, of course, Father. Well, it has been—many years since my last confession. There's quite a bit to talk about."

"Just relax, Joe. Anything you say is between me, you, and God. There can be no secrets, for He already knows all. This is for your benefit."

Unnoticed by Perrone, Craig touched a small button on the underside of his desk. Something, somewhere began a low humming noise, just barely perceptible there in the office. Joe did not notice it, nor did he notice a faint odor that soon pervaded the room. Or, if he did, he paid it no mind. Craig held his breath for a time and held a handkerchief over his mouth and nose.

"I have done things," Perrone said. "I have taken lives. I chose to do so, and I cannot truly say that I repent of any of it. I have taken the law into my own hand—man's law, and God's too, perhaps. I believed, and still do, that what I have done is right. I do not seek advice, or even absolution, to be honest. I merely wish to confess."

"Go on, Joseph. Unburden yourself."

As Perrone talked, he felt as though he were drifting away from his own body somehow.

"I have created for myself a second identity in order to carry out these activities. Man's law is insufficient in many cases, particularly when it has been corrupted by evil. And God does not allow Himself to intervene. He leaves that up to us, as we follow the dictates of conscience."

"There's more to tell, Joe," Craig said, his voice a dark caress. "You mustn't keep anything back from me, for the good of your soul."

"Yes, you're right, of course. Everything seems very clear to me now, father. You will remember when my family died. Criminals murdered them, then burned down our house. I was the only one who survived. I don't know why, exactly. I think my brother had something to do with it."

"Anthony."

"Yes. He got me out, but he went back in for some reason. I don't know why. He burned with my mother and father. But our parents had been shot before they burned, the police said. So they didn't burn to death, at least. But Anthony..."

"Never mind Anthony," Craig said. "We are talking about you. What happened to you?"

"Well, I drifted for a while, I didn't know what to do with myself, I had plenty of money. And, eventually, I made a decision."

"And what was that?"

"To become the Bay Phantom. The newspapers gave me that name. I thought of myself as no one at all, you see. That's why I wear the mask. I fight criminals. I kill some of them."

"Tell me, do you do all of this by yourself, or have you involved others?"

"I have friends, yes, and they assist me."

"That's good. Friends are good, Joseph. Now, I want you to tell me about them. Please tell me *all* about them, Joseph..."

After Joe Perrone took his leave, Archbishop Craig sat silently in his chair for half an hour. Perrone would remember very little about his confession. The effects of the gas would fade, along with most of his memories. Craig thought about everything he had heard.

Presently, he stood up, turned off the lights, went to the closet door behind the desk, and opened it.

"Something has come up, Kraken," the Archbishop said. "We may have a problem, or we may have a solution, I'm not sure which."

"Tell me," came a low croak from the darkness.

"I just had a visit from an old parishioner of mine, young Joseph Perrone. Under the seal of the Confessional, he revealed some very interesting things."

"I am aware. I was here, Craig."

"Of course. You are always here."

"We need to have a look at all the information we possess on the Bay Phantom. And on Joseph Perrone. Then we need to correlate the two, and draw some conclusions."

"As you say, Kraken."

CHAPTER ELEVEN
GUTS

"Not many people survive a disembowelment," the doctor said. "You're a very lucky young lady."

"I'm not that young," Winona Dirge replied. "And you've got a funny idea of luck."

This was a new doctor, one she had never seen before. She had been told that her recovery was complete. She had the idea that this fellow had heard of her case and just had to see for himself.

"All right," the doctor said with a mechanical smile and an almost-imperceptible nod. "Not lucky in the traditional sense, then. But, for someone whose internal organs once spent a significant amount of time outside of her body, extraordinarily so."

Winona had lost her gall bladder, one kidney, and several feet of intestine. Nothing she couldn't manage without and she felt oddly better for being rid of it. Poor Milt had always believed in traveling light.

But poor Milt was gone. Milton Cabal, the legendary assassin, "The Most Dangerous Man in the World."

Ever since he had been killed, and she nearly so, she had been in this hospital. How long had it been? Several weeks at least. More like several months, probably. But she had purposely neglected to keep track of the time. During her early days here, she had been in and out of consciousness, delirious and in a great deal of pain whenever she was awake. There had been surgeries, feeding tubes, pain medication, and therapy.

"Yeah," Winona said. "I don't think they were all that spent time outside my body."

"I beg your pardon?"

"Never mind, I'm sorry, go ahead."

"Of course," the doctor went on, "you required almost eighteen hours of surgery, but it wouldn't have been possible at all if the damage had not been so remarkably limited. None of your organs were damaged by whatever cut through your skin and muscle tissue, and their integrity relative to one another was intact in spite of the—ah, spillage."

A nurse stepped into the room. "There's someone here to see you, Miss Mayfair. I can send her away if you'd rather not—"

"No, it's okay. Who the hell would want to see me? Well, tell whoever it is to come on in."

The doctor walked out, leaving Winona alone. She wondered what was up. It was probably some kind of cop. Well, she couldn't be connected with anything, as far as she knew, and she had no intention of answering any dumb questions.

The police had already spoken with her about the events at the funeral home. They had taken her fingerprints, which had come back as belonging to one Delores Mayfair, a schoolteacher from Des Moines Iowa. She had no criminal record; her prints were only on file in Washington because she had once applied for a job on an Army base.

All of that chicanery had been accomplished by Milt years ago. When the cops in Mobile, and a few feds as well, had asked her how she had come to be in that place, she simply told them she did not know. They finally decided that she had been kidnapped like some of the other poor girls who had been victims of a sinister group called the International Patriots Guild. She allowed the authorities to form the impression that she had come to the Gulf Coast from Iowa in hopes of finding some kind of unspecified opportunity, but had drifted instead into prostitution. She didn't care what they thought about her, so long as they left her alone.

The real story was downright incredible, and would certainly tend to incriminate her. As professional assassins, she and Milt had become involved with a gangster named Penny Carter and a super-criminal called Doctor Piranha. Winona and Milt had agreed to aid Penny Carter in her assault on the Patriots Guild. The final confrontation, in the Donner-Purdy Funeral Home in Mobile, had ended with Milt dead and Winona gutted, more or less by accident, by one of Penny's other "assets," a superhuman psychopath known as the Werewolf.

"Excuse me," said the nurse, tapping with a pencil on the open door. "Your visitor is here."

In the doorway stood a young black woman. Her skin was very dark. In the dim hospital light, only her eyes were clearly visible. They were filled with both joy and apprehension. Winona looked at her for a couple of seconds before recognition dawned.

"Why, it's... It's *you*," Winona said, smiling. "How are you?"

"I'm okay," said Mirabelle Darcy, taking a couple of tentative steps into the room. "I'm more worried about how *you* are."

"More or less in one piece again. I don't feel too bad at all, really."

"That's good." The woman was silent for a few seconds, then she said, "You know, I never really introduced myself. My name's Mirabelle. Mirabelle Darcy."

"That's a nice name."

Mirabelle Darcy seemed flustered, as though she had no idea what to say, or whether she should say anything. "I swear, I thought you were dead, Winona," she blurted out. "I wouldn't have just left you there if—"

Winona smiled at her. "I know, Mirabelle, I understand. It's okay. I *shouldn't* have survived that, I don't know how I—"

"The men that came to clean up after that—thing at the funeral home," Mirabelle interrupted, with tears in her eyes, "they found you alive, and I didn't learn about it until—"

"It's okay, Mirabelle, really."

"I feel like I got you into all that, and—"

"Mirabelle—"

"And then I was afraid to come see you because I felt responsible, but I kept track of you, and—"

"*Mirabelle! Shut up!* It wasn't your fault. I'm not clear on what happened, but it was Doctor Piranha and that redhead that were responsible, I know. Look, I survived, and I feel pretty good, actually. I'm still sore, but I have less junk under the bonnet. They tossed out a few pounds of meat I didn't need, and—"

Mirabelle shuddered, then smiled—her way of dismissing the unpleasant images. "So, what are you going to do now? If you need to get in touch with some friends—"

"Well, I don't really have any friends. Or family, before you bring up *that* word. All I had was Milt, and now—Well, at least I'm not wanted. By the law, or... by anybody."

Mirabelle, who had been gnawing at her lower lip, said, "If you'd like—I mean, if you want me to, I'd like to be your friend."

"Really? You would?"

Mirabelle nodded. "Sure. If you'd like, you can come stay at my place until you figure out, y'know, what you're going to do and all."

"Hm. Well, maybe that would be a good idea. I don't really know what—I mean, I don't think I'm gonna stay in the assassin business, not all by myself. Hell, do you know I've never actually killed anybody?"

"Really? I... I did, once. I didn't much care for it, even though the guy deserved it."

Winona nodded. "Yeah. A lot of people deserve it. I just never gave it to any of them." She smiled crookedly. "I always wanted to give it so some creep who *really* deserved it. Some fearsome assassin I am, eh?"

"Aw, you're okay," Mirabelle said. "Look, I'm gonna go talk to your doctor about your release."

It took an hour to get everything settled. Mirabelle arranged for Winona's bill to be paid. On the drive to Tull House, Mirabelle gave Winona a bit of disinformation and a few instructions.

Mirabelle explained that, while she did important work for a masked adventurer called the Bay Phantom, of whom Winona might have heard (she had), she was employed by a man named Joe Perrone. Perrone was in on the whole Bay Phantom thing, but there were things he did not need to know. Chief among these was the fact that Mirabelle had broken into Leavenworth Federal Prison and broken Doctor Piranha out. That was when Mirabelle and Winona had met. She and her partner, Milt Cabal, had been sent to Leavenworth, ostensibly to kill Piranha. In fact, the situation had been more complicated than that. Perrone, Mirabelle said, did not need to know anything about it. In fact, everything to do with the breakout, the subsequent trip to Mobile, and anything that had happened before, after, during, as a consequence of, or ancillary to any of that was off-limits.

"That stuff has to remain between us girls," Mirabelle said. "I can't explain it all to you, but I've got good reasons for it."

"I'm sure you do. I had to do the same kind of thing with poor old Milt. Men have to think they're in charge and know everything that's going on. It would kill 'em if they knew the truth."

"Boy, would it ever."

"Look, Mirabelle. I appreciate you doing all this for me. But if it's just because you feel guilty—"

"No, that's not it. I mean, I do feel sort of guilty, but—Look, Winona, that fact is, I don't have very many friends, either. And I—Well, I *like* you, okay? That's all, I just like you."

"Okay. That's good. I like you too."

They fell silent then, both of them smiling to themselves.

After a few minutes of looking out the window and taking in the passing scenery, Winona said, "You know, I lived in Mobile for a short while when I was a girl."

"Really? No, I didn't know that."

"It was only for a year. My father was in the Army, we moved around a lot."

She thought of the time she had spent here, the Catholic school she had attended, the boy she had had a crush on. He was a strange one, to be sure. He had liked her too, but seemed to be under the influence of a slightly older boy who seemed to be up to some kind of unknown mischief.

Still, he had gone out of his way to spend time with her. When she had announced to the class that she would soon be moving away again, he had asked her to meet him in the cloakroom, where he had given her a kiss, her first.

Before she left, he had told her that they would meet again one day, that the things that would happen to them in life would bring them together again at some point. Very romantic, especially for such a young kid, but total bullshit, of course. She had never seen him again. It was a nice memory, though.

Certainly, it was more pleasant than everything that had happened to her afterwards. The conflicts with her father, who had wanted a boy and been stuck with a girl. She had tried to please him, to prove herself, and failed with every effort. It was while she was attending a university in Milwaukee that she had met Milt Cabal. His ambition had been to become a highly-paid assassin, and she had joined him. She had affected to use a sword, to set herself apart from others in her new trade.

And look where all that had led her. Manipulated by criminals and gutted by a werewolf. Life had failed to live up to her expectations, and vice versa.

Well, perhaps it had all been worthwhile. At least now, finally, she had something that felt like it might become a genuine friendship.

"Are you ready to break some laws to get Tom Dart out of prison alive?" Mirabelle asked Joe Perrone. They were seated at the kitchen table in Tull House, their favorite spot to talk, argue, and ruminate. Perrone was sipping at a grape Nehi, while Mirabelle held a glass of wine.

Winona had been installed in a room on the second floor of Tull House. Mirabelle had given Perrone a very creative explanation for Mirabelle's relationship to the woman and the reasons for her presence here now.

Perrone, who trusted Mirabelle implicitly, did not question any of it, which caused her some distress, but she was learning to live with that. There were so many things she could never tell him about Doctor Piranha and her own activities involving him. She didn't like it, but she could live with it for Perrone's sake.

"Of course I am," said Perrone. "I suppose I might as well break as many laws as I please, since I'm a wanted man. And Tom is innocent. The law is mistaken, corrupted."

"Right. But I'm not just talking about the laws of man, Joe, I'm talking about the laws of nature."

"Mirabelle..."

"Okay, maybe I'm overdramatizing. But I've been thinking about it, and I've got a way to get him out, and I think it's the *only* thing that'll work."

"Yes, this plan of yours. Are you ready to give me the details?"

"Yes, I am," she said. "I've been experimenting."

"On whom?"

"Not people. Mice."

"Oh, Mirabelle, you know how I—"

Perrone had recently discovered in himself a great fondness for mice. He kept several of them in cages in one of the secret rooms under Tull House. He doted on them, fussed over them, and generally treated them as though they were tiny people.

"Yes, I know how do. But it's okay. I didn't kill any of them. Well, I did kill *one*, sort of, but he's okay now."

"You're not making any sense."

"Yes, I am. Listen to me, and I'll explain."

An hour and a half later, Perrone sat staring at the wall on the opposite side of the room, saying nothing.

"Well?" Mirabelle prompted him. "What do you say?"

He thought for a moment, then said, "If anyone else proposed such a thing to me, I would have him or her taken to the nearest psychiatric hospital for a full evaluation."

"So would I, if it was anybody but me. But it'll work, I'm sure of it. Also, it's the only chance we have at this point."

"Indeed."

"We can explain it to Maizie Dart—maybe in a little less detail—and she can help us prepare."

"All right, Mirabelle. Proceed."

CHAPTER TWELVE
THE EMBALMER AND PAUL

Rather like a doting parent, The Embalmer was proud of the progress Paul had made. The man was virtually back to normal, though large portions of his memory were gone, perhaps forever. He claimed not to recall his surname, but the Embalmer had doubts on that score. He had the feeling the old man was holding onto that information for some reason.

Well, it was his own business, after all. *I have my own secrets too*, he reasoned. *Some of them I even keep from myself.*

The Embalmer's memory could best be described as a constantly-shifting scrap yard, filled with shadowy and puzzling objects—probably owing to the many chemical experiments he had carried out on his own person through the years. What *was* the name of that kid that had gotten him started on all that, way back when? Andrew or Antoine or something along those lines.

The Embalmer wondered what had become of the lad. Nothing good, he was sure.

As for Paul, that was quite a story in itself. A few months ago, the Embalmer had been staying in a little clinic over in Baldwin County, as a "guest" of the Bay Phantom. There, he had talked to doctors and received various medications. He suspected that the Phantom was trying to "reform" him, though he doubted such a thing was possible, at least not in the way the Phantom had in mind.

Paul had been brought to the clinic around the same time as the Embalmer. He had been in pretty rough shape. According to the Phantom, the old man had been held captive by members of the Ku Klux Klan for many years, and his mind had given way. Minds, the Embalmer knew, were like that. Apply too much pressure, and they tended to fold.

One day, a group of armed thugs had shown up, intent on kidnapping Paul. Paul had been brought into the clinic shortly after the Embalmer had been installed there, and he had been a basket case at the time. He could not communicate at all, and could barely look after himself in the most basic ways. The Phantom had explained that the old man had been rescued from the clutches of the Ku Klux Klan, who had held him prisoner for years, for reasons which were not entirely clear. Unfortunately for the would-be kidnappers, the Embalmer had thwarted their attempt and had escaped from the clinic himself, taking Paul along for safekeeping.

For months now, he had been working with his "patient," and Paul had shown remarkable improvement. The Embalmer felt that the old man was almost ready for the role that destiny had surely selected for him: assistant and confidante to the Embalmer in his new career as a crime-fighter.

"We need to talk about some things, Paul," he told the old man one morning over the breakfast table in the little house they'd been using as a hideaway since February. "Now that you're more *compos mentis* than you were when first we met, there are a few things you need to understand about your benefactor."

"Okay,' said Paul. "I'll admit you're something of a puzzlement to me. I can think a lot straighter now, but I don't remember too much. I mean, I know my name, but I don't really recall anything about myself or my life."

"I'm afraid I can't help you there. But we were talking about *me*, and I can provide a little more enlightenment on that subject, though my past is a bit murky to me—so we do have that in common, which may be why Providence has brought us together, though I can't really speak for the ethereal forces, you understand."

"I guess so."

"Yes, that's all we can do, is to guess." The Embalmer shook his head slowly. "Anyhow, my earliest years are veiled in obscurity and uncertainty, but I vividly recall the last decade or so, and it isn't a pretty story, Paul, not at all. It is a tale of criminality and depravity so lurid and unsavory as to beggar the wan and timorous imaginations of decent churchgoing folk. Or is that an oxymoron? Well, be that as it may, you must know as much of the truth as I am able to piece together for you."

"All right. You know, there's something kind of weird about you. I don't mean just the obvious. There's something kind of otherworldly. Of course, you might just be really, really crazy, and that's what makes you seem that way."

The Embalmer laughed. "That's one of the things I like about you, Paul. You say what's on your mind. Back when we first met, and you had practically no mind at all, you said nothing. Now that your intellect is making a comeback, your observations are pithy and entertaining. You remind me of my other friend, the one that wears the mask, though he lacks your clarity of vision sometimes. Too caught up in the morality of his actions, you see."

Paul shook his head. "No, I really don't see, but I'm getting used to that. You may have clarity of vision, but you don't make much sense a lot of the time."

"That seems to be my grand tradition, Paul. I seldom make sense to myself, if I'm honest, and yet I persevere. And that is what I wish to discuss with you today, the next step in my personal evolution. I have spoken often of my masked friend, the Bay Phantom. As you know, he is a self-styled crime fighter. And I have been a self-styled criminal, beholden to no one but myself. I have done it, and, if I may say so myself, done a good job of it. And now it is time for a change."

"You gonna turn yourself in?"

"Good Lord, no! What would that accomplish?"

"Well, you could sort of pay for your transgressions."

"Oh my goodness, no," the Embalmer said, pulling a sour face and shaking his head. "I'm not interested in paying for anything. I don't keep a ledger, Paul, and my transgressions, if any, are my own affair. I just need a change. I want to do something different. The idea of fighting crime for no reason and no reward appeals to me, and that is the course I have set for my future. *Our* future, Paul, if you'd care to join me. You see, I used to think of my friend, the Phantom, as a lone wolf of sorts, like myself, but I have learned that that is not the case. He has a helper or a partner if you prefer, and that is something I have always lacked. Except for when I was younger. There was another boy, a year or so older than me, who helped me with my chemical researches. But that was a long time ago—I think."

"I see," said Paul. "Well, you've been good to me, and I do owe you a lot. You seem like a good guy to me, all things considered. Whatever it is you've got planned, if you're on the right road, I'm with you."

Paul had not been entirely forthright with his odd benefactor. While much of his past was murky, he remembered things that had happened to him before he had fallen into the hands of Hector Sams. Sams, believing that Paul possessed some kind of supernatural power—having managed to survive a lynching by Sams and his K.K.K. cronies—held him captive, in a cage, for almost two decades. Paul's memory had withered and almost died.

But now he remembered his family: his wife, Eugenia, and his daughter, Mirabelle.

His wife, he now knew, was dead. On one of his rare trips outside the Embalmer's little house, he had visited the public library and gone through several years' worth of newspaper obituaries, and found Eugenia's among them.

In his earlier life, before Hector Sams and the Klan, Paul had dabbled a bit in hoodoo, folk magic, and vodun. Not that he was an adept, or even much of a believer, but he had always found such things intriguing, and had discovered that there was genuine power in things most educated people regarded as mere superstition.

He had become interested in the phenomenon of ghostly hauntings, and had pursued his own personal course of investigation. Over a period of years, he had established to his own satisfaction that the things people called "ghosts" actually did exist, though he had no idea what they actually were. He had established a method of communicating with them, for all it was worth. They really didn't have much to say that made any sense. They were disembodied, damaged intellects, intelligent to a degree, but hopelessly addled.

One evening while the Embalmer was out, Paul had gotten himself into the proper frame of mind for communication with the entities, and attempted to make contact. Nothing happened for almost an hour. Then, a soft, sibilant sound drifted through the room, gradually growing louder and clearer, until it seemed there were hundreds of voices, all whispering the same thing.

Mister Paul Mister Paul it has been a long time you are better now you are better we know we are glad it is good it is good

"Yes, it's good to hear you again too. It has been too long. I want to ask you some questions. Are you up to it?"

Yes yes ask us ask us

"You know I got a daughter, her name is Mirabelle. I think she used to talk to y'all too. Do you know anything about her, how she's doing?"

Miss Mirabelle yes she is fine we talk to her Miss Mirabelle she is a good woman she talks to us, she is kind

"That's true, she always was. I'm glad she still talks with you. How are things with her? Does she have any, you know friends?"

Joe is her friend she loves him he loves her they protect one another from things that might hurt them

"Joe? Do you mean little Joey Perrone? Well, he wouldn't be little now. They still hanging around together?"

Perrone Perrone yes Joe Perrone Joe wears a mask we're not supposed to tell anyone Mirabelle said not to but you're her daddy

"Wears a mask, huh? Now, that's awfully interesting. Makes sense too. Lots of things make more sense now. Thanks. Thanks very much."

CHAPTER THIRTEEN
THE SHAMBLING MEN

It was a little past midnight, in a second-floor apartment in a brick building on Conti Street. The flat was shared by two of the Bay Phantom's agents, Shorty Red and Louis Rickert.

Louis was seated at the little dining table, tongue protruding from his mouth, laboriously pushing a pencil across a sheet of lined yellow paper.

"What are you doing?" Shorty Red asked. There was nothing short or red about the man. He was a heavily-muscled giant, nearly seven feet tall, with pale skin and close-cropped white hair. He was only in his thirties; his hair had been colorless ever since he was a child.

"Writing a letter," Louis replied. He was an average fellow—average height and weight, neither handsome nor ugly, with unremarkable brown hair and eyes. "What's it look like I'm doing? Knitting a sweater?"

"Who are you writing a letter to?"

"Alice Tague, if it's any of your business, which it ain't."

Alice Tague was a former prostitute, a friend of Louis' who had played a pivotal role in the destruction of the horrible Cannibal Guild months before. The poor girl had been ill, in need of treatment, and thanks to the reward she had received for the recapture of Doctor Piranha, she had been able to move to Huntsville to receive it. Louis seemed to have become smitten with her, which, in Shorty's opinion, was a great improvement over his earlier hopeless infatuation with Gladys Turnbull.

"Well, well," Shorty said impishly. "A love letter?"

"Hell, no. Just a friendly letter. Say, Shorty, how do you spell 'adore?' Is it like a door that you walk through?"

"In a way I suppose it is, but the word is spelled a-d-o-r-e."

"No kidding? How 'bout that! Words are funny things."

"They can be."

Louis continued his labors, scratching away with his pencil, tongue protruding from the side of his mouth. Shorty browsed his bookshelf for a while, then walked over to the window to have a look down on the street below.

"What the devil is going on out there?" he grumbled, raising the sash.

"What is it?" Louis asked, laying the pencil aside.

"Come have a look at this," said Shorty.

Louis joined him, peering around the giant's shoulder.

"Jesus," he said, "looks like a bunch of rummies are going on a rampage!"

Indeed it did. Fully a dozen men, all of them obvious derelicts—shabby clothes, unshaved faces, gaunt frames—swarming up the middle of the street and spilling over onto the sidewalks on both sides. All of them were equipped with objects that could easily become instruments of mayhem: a couple of long-bladed knives, a baseball bat, a two-by-four with nails sticking out of it, and so on.

There were no other people on the street apart from the strange crew, and they were taking out whatever grievances they might have on inanimate objects. One of them pounded a mailbox several times with a length of lead pipe, another shattered a shop window with his bare fist. One of them threw a brick at a small yellow cat and missed.

"Get on the phone," Shorty said. "The Boss'll want to know about this, I think."

Louis dashed over to the telephone table, snatched up the instrument, and hastily dialed a number. Somewhere, in some mysterious place he couldn't even imagine, a phone rang, and was answered within seconds.

"Yes?" came a clipped, muffled voice. Louis was pretty sure it was a woman, and he was pretty sure he'd met her before. But he didn't wonder too much about the Boss' private business, at least not out loud.

"Hey, this is Agent Rickert reporting. The Boss needs to get over to our location on Conti Street, we got some kind of a bum riot going on."

"You've got a—? Never mind, he's nearby, I'll send him right over. I assume Shorty is with you? Well, keep an eye on the situation, but don't do anything drastic, hear?"

"Yes'm, that's a ten-four. Agent Rickert over and out." He hung up. Turning to Shorty, he said, "The voice told me the Boss is coming and you and me are supposed to keep an eye on the situation but to not do nothing drastic, hear?"

The Boss strangely disapproved of the casual use of lethal force. Louis wasn't too fond of it himself, but there was an element of self-preservation involved. If someone was trying to kill him, he figured he had a right to kill them back.

"We'd better go down there," Shorty said.

"I dunno, that seems kinda drastic. We got a window up here, don't we? We can keep an eye on 'em through it."

"That one with the red hair is hefting a tire iron and heading toward my car," Shorty replied. "I'm not having that."

"Oh boy, here we go."

They grabbed their guns, just in case, and headed down the stairs and out onto the street. All of the men stopped whatever pointless acts of mayhem they had been up to, and turned to look at Shorty and Louis.

They were scary. Louis had seen depraved men before, men in the grip of illness or madness, but none had ever frightened him as these did.

They looked like they were dead, apart from the fact that they were moving and creating a disturbance. Their movements were jerky, though, and stiff. They were like marionettes that had not been well cared-for.

And then there were the eyes. Totally vacant, as though there were no one and nothing living behind them.

There was something supernatural about it, that's what. They were like those creeps in that movie "White Zombie."

They moved toward Shorty and Louis, arms outstretched. Some of them held weapons, others did not.

Shorty had stowed his pistol away and was keeping the men away from him by stiff-arming them backwards, while trying to come up with a strategy for nabbing one of them without hurting the poor devil too badly, and without getting hurt himself.

Louis, meanwhile, was dashing back and forth, avoiding contact, his hand on the pistol in his jacket pocket, flirting with the idea of shooting just one of the lunatics, in the leg or something, to send a sort of message to the others. Not that they seemed to have sense enough to receive any messages...

A car tore around the nearest corner and screeched to a stop in the middle of the street. The vagrants didn't seem to notice. From it leapt the Bay Phantom.

"Stand back, fellows!" the masked man yelled, in that calm, reasonable way he had of yelling. You never felt like you were being yelled at, but you still knew he meant business. Louis and Shorty moved away from the men nearest them.

The Phantom looked up, and, sure enough, there were those mysterious little globes of light, floating and bobbing about twenty feet above the street.

He was holding what looked like a kid's BB gun, with a large, cylindrical magazine attached in front of the trigger guard, and what looked like a little oxygen tank bolted to the stock. The barrel was very wide, about three inches in diameter.

"Hold your breath, fellows," he said to Shorty and Louis.

The Phantom pulled the trigger three times in rapid succession, slightly adjusting his aim each time.

PAFF! PAFF! PAFF!

Three small canisters shot from the barrel of the weapon, each one striking one of the men in the chest. The canisters burst open, releasing a thick, yellow vapor.

The Phantom stood back, waiting for the powerful anesthetic gas to take effect.

But it didn't.

"What on earth?" the Phantom breathed puzzled.

The shambling men continued to move, but they ignored the Phantom, instead the swarmed over Shorty and Louis.

The masked man was about to take a hand when his attention was arrested by a loud voice.

"There he is!"

Two men had come around the corner. One was unusually tall, almost as tall as the hulking Shorty Red, but as thin as a consumptive. The man's face was utterly lifeless, pale white, with no more expression than a pan of brackish water. The contours of the skull showed through the thin white skin, reminding the Phantom of an uncomfortable piece of furniture covered with a white sheet.

The other was very short, no more than five feet, two inches.

They were, of course, the pair that had committed the murders on Durant Street.

The tall man interlaced the fingers of both hands and cracked his knuckles.

"Come on, Mister Bay Phantom, let's see just how tough you are."

The Phantom shook his head slightly in disgust. Some people just felt that they had something to prove.

He holstered the gas canister gun and stepped forward to confront the tall man. Without any warning, the gangly fellow dashed forward and

"Hold your breath, fellows."

planted a solid right in the Phantom's stomach, doubling him over and nearly knocking him off of his feet.

The masked man got his balance, prevented himself from pitching over, and back pedaled a few steps. This was going to be more difficult than he had anticipated.

The tall man moved like a suit full of water, rather than a solid, articulated body. The Phantom had studied and practiced every form of hand-to-hand combat imaginable, but none of it had prepared him for this.

The man must be double or triple jointed, if there were even any bones in there at all. When the masked man did manage to land a blow, it felt like he was punching a sack of straw.

The man's fists were another story. He landed several punches to the Phantom's torso, and they felt like sledgehammer blows.

"You think you're something," the man said. "Well, we're on to you and all your little helpers too."

"What?" the Phantom asked, startled by the remark.

The man did not explain any further. They traded a few more blows, the tall man's connecting solidly, the Phantom's having no effect. Shorty and Louis could only watch, as they struggled with their mindless opponents.

The Phantom took quite a beating, and inflicted no discernable damage at all on the tall man.

Since the hand-to-hand wasn't going too well, the Phantom decided to try the only other option he had short of lethal force. Stepping back, he pulled the gas canister gun from its holster, aimed the contraption at his opponent, and pulled the trigger

PAFF!

The small canister struck the man in the chest. It didn't knock him out, but it didn't do him any favors, either. He staggered backward and moved in a circle, holding a hand over his mouth and nose.

As the man twisted around, the Phantom noticed for the first time that he had something strapped to his back.

"All right, Mouse!" the tall man shouted. "We've made our point! Let's wrap this up!"

The shambling men ceased harrying Shorty and Louis and stepped away.

The small man had a pair of automatics, one in each hand.

"Beat it, you mugs!" he shouted, pointing the guns at the Phantom's men.

"Do as he says, fellows!" the Phantom commanded. "Get yourselves to safety!"

Meanwhile, the tall man had taken the brief opportunity to deploy the thing he had strapped to his back—an army-grade flamethrower. He raised the nozzle, attached by a heavy hose to a pair of metal tanks, and depressed the mechanism, sending a sputtering jet of flame at the derelicts.

The Phantom dropped his gas gun and pulled a revolver from inside his jacket.

"That's enough from you," the Phantom said, drawing a bead on the tall man's head. There rose in him the cold conviction that this man ought to die, here and now, and he was prepared to make it happen.

A bullet whizzed past the masked man's head. He had forgotten about the short fellow! He turned his head and saw the little man rushing at him, getting off another shot that the Phantom just managed to duck under.

He took aim at the short man, and, when less than three feet separated them, the Phantom fired.

The short man fell to the pavement, shot through the chest. The Phantom turned back to where the tall man had been, but the fellow had vanished.

The police chose that moment to arrive. The tall man was gone, and Shorty and Louis had ducked out of sight somewhere, so only the Bay Phantom remained there on the street with the unconscious killer and the burning corpses.

Three police cars skidded to a stop, disgorging four uniformed officers and one plainclothes man.

"Put your hands up!" Detective Lieutenant Matranga commanded. He had a revolver in his hand.

The Phantom complied. As Matranga moved closer, the masked man spoke to him:

"I can't allow you to apprehend me, you know."

"I ain't really worried about what you can't allow, buddy. We have orders to shoot on sight. I'm trying to be civilized about this, but—"

"I know. I'm sorry. But it won't hurt, I promise you. Just relax."

"Now look here..."

The Bay Phantom clenched his raised hands into fists. There was a muffled noise, like a small explosion, and the world went black.

Later on, Matranga figured it out. The masked man had detonated some kind of smoke bomb that filled that section of the street with a thick, black haze. It only lasted a few seconds before the breeze carried it away, but that was more than enough time for the Phantom to find his car and leave the scene.

Some of the shambling men had escaped the burning, and were found wandering aimlessly several blocks from the scene of the action. All of them had been brought to headquarters.

The small man had been taken to the hospital, where a slug had been removed from the spot where it had lodged between two ribs. The bullet had entered the man's chest on the right side, broken two ribs there, and traveled on to the back, stopping about two inches from the spinal cord. Nothing vital had been punctured, though the impact had caused the left lung to partially collapse, necessitating treatment. Once he was patched up and conscious, twelve hours later, he was taken to police headquarters, where he refused to say a word. He was being held on "suspicion of involvement in an affray resulting in loss of life." Lieutenant Matranga wasn't sure how long the man could be held on such an ambiguous charge. The chief seemed to be of the opinion that the little man had been nothing more than an innocent bystander, ruthlessly gunned down by the Bay Phantom.

"I know this bird," Eliot Ness said. He and Matranga were standing in the dingy hallway outside the little holding cell where the man sat staring at the grimy gray wall. "His name's Mark Mills. They called him the Mouse back in Chicago."

Matranga peeped through the tiny window in the cell door at the immobile figure. "He's from Chicago?"

Ness nodded. "Used to work for Capone. Part of the inner circle, in fact, Big Al's Praetorian Guard. He is, as Thomas Hobbes once said about life itself, nasty, brutish, and short. The Mouse disappeared around the time Capone got sent up, along with his partner—a psycho by the name of Jack Foregone."

"Never heard of either one of them," Matranga said.

“You wouldn’t have. They didn’t exactly court publicity. But, between the two of them, they had a bigger body count than any ten hoodlums put together.”

“You think this Foregone character might be down here now?”

“Well, the two of them were inseparable. If the Mouse is here, odds are the Scarecrow is too.”

“Scarecrow?”

“Yeah, that’s what they called Foregone. Big, gangly galoot, thin as a broomstick. But strong, and mean. Not just mean, he’s crazy. He and the Mouse here worked for Capone more for love of the job than money. They like cutting people up.”

“Is that a fact?” Matranga said thoughtfully, rubbing the side of his nose.

“It is,” Ness said.

“So, on the one hand, we’ve got those skells in the tank. Those guys ain’t gonna say anything. The doc says there’s something the matter with them, like they were drugged or something. The two that are being charged with the murders the other night, and the rest of ‘em—the way we found them wandering around after the business on Conti Street, they weren’t headed anywhere. They don’t seem to be part of any organized gang. But these are supposed to be our mastermind killers.”

Ness nodded.

“And, on the other hand,” Matranga continued, “we’ve got a couple of guys from Chicago who cut people up because they like doing it.”

“Yeah,” Ness said. He was thoughtful too. “And then there’s the Bay Phantom. He’s either involved in this or he knows something about who’s really behind it. Either way, I’d sure like to talk to him. I don’t know that I believe he was involved in any killings. But the mayor and your chief sure have decided he was. Him and those whacked-out bums. That’s kind of funny, don’t you think?”

Matranga just shrugged.

“I think you know more about what goes on in this town than you let on,” Ness went on. “And I think maybe you don’t like it too much. I approached you for a reason, you know. I did some checking before I came down here. I can sniff out a dirty cop pretty easy—and once in a while, I can sniff out a clean one. Do you know what I’m saying?”

Matranga was silent for a long time. Thinking, weighing options and probabilities. He had almost reached a certain brink, and he opened his mouth and drew breath to step over it. But then he remembered who he was and where he was.

"Naw," he said. "I really don't know what you're saying, Mister Ness."

Ness was silent for a few moments, frustrated by the opportunity that had just slipped away.

"Well, Matranga, I can tell you this," he said grimly. "As long as the Mouse is alive, the Scarecrow will try to get him out of your custody. I would recommend putting some extra guards on him."

"That was a close one," Mirabelle observed. She and Perrone were down in one of the rooms beneath Tull House, the one equipped as an infirmary. Mirabelle was patching up the injuries Perrone had sustained in the battle with the strange tall man.

"Yes," Perrone agreed, "rather too close. Sadly, though, I am no closer to knowing what is going on. Something the tall man said bothered me. He made a remark about 'all my little helpers.' Why did they show up on that particular street? Do you think that group, or whatever they were, knew that Louis and Shorty live there?"

"I don't see how they could. I also don't see how they couldn't. In other words, I have no idea."

"Best to assume they did, to be on the safe side. I'll have the boys relocate for the time being. And there's something else. As far as my 'little helpers' are concerned, Gladys will need to be careful too. I'll speak with her. And Tom Dart could be included in that group."

"Tom Dart is locked up."

"Yes, but his wife and daughter aren't. I just have this awful feeling, Mirabelle—I'm going to have Shorty and Louis keep an eye on Tom's family, I think. That will get them out of their apartment, *and* put them to good use. I'll have to speak with Mrs. Dart very soon at any rate, once I figure out how to explain things to her. We'll need her help to rescue Tom."

"Uh-huh." Mirabelle, finished with her work on Perrone's person, turned her attention to his Bay Phantom suit, which lay spread out on a table.

"Well, this doesn't look so bad," she said. "Nothing got torn this time. It's a little dirty." She picked up the trousers and felt the pockets.

"You ought to stop carrying all this money in your pocket," she said. "Someone's liable to knock you in the head and take it."

Perrone laughed. "Mirabelle," he said, "sometimes that roll of bills is the greatest weapon in my arsenal. You'd be surprised how often bribes prove more effective than fists."

"No I wouldn't."

"And sometimes I need to buy things on the fly. Also, I am forever running into poor unfortunates who can use a bit of help."

"Sure. Well, I don't suppose any harm will ever come of it."

CHAPTER FOURTEEN

MAIZIE

Two nights after the debacle on Conti Street, while Perrone was trying to decide on the best way to approach Maizie Dart, the matter was taken out of his hands. Mirabelle answered a telephone call that came through the Phantom's special radio line, and handed it over to Perrone.

"It's them crazy bums again, Boss," Louis said, once he was speaking to his mysterious employer. "More of them. They're just kind of hanging around outside Mrs. Dart's house. It's like they're waiting on something."

"Thank you, Louis. You and Shorty stand by. Don't do anything unless they approach the house. If they do, you may use any means necessary to stop them."

Tom's house was in a quiet residential neighborhood, neither shabby nor particularly classy, in the Crichton area. There was no opulence here, nor was there squalor. Most of the houses were fairly new, nestled together in neat rows beneath the ubiquitous live oaks that stood in almost every yard and reaching out over the streets, limbs heavy with dark leaves.

The Dart residence was a small, one-story, two-bedroom bungalow, no more than twenty years old.

Shorty's sedan was parked across the street. The Phantom brought his own automobile to a stop behind it and got out. Louis and Shorty were standing by the curb. Six men stood like statues on the far edge of the Darts' lawn.

"See, Boss, they're just standing there," Louis whispered.

"At least two of them have knives," Shorty added in an undertone.

"Ominous," remarked the Phantom. "Well, perhaps we had best round them up, see if any of them will talk."

"I really doubt that they *can* talk," Shorty said.

"I fear you're right, Shorty, but perhaps we can learn something from them just the same."

At that moment, the standing, staring men snapped to life, as though suddenly galvanized, and began a rapid advance toward the little house.

"Aw, shit, here we go," Louis moaned.

"Steady on, Louis," the Phantom said, drawing an automatic from a hidden holster. "Let's move, men."

The trio cautiously advanced toward the group of shambling figures, several of whom were now brandishing long-bladed knives. Whoever had outfitted them had apparently selected a motley collection of mismatched kitchen blades.

The Phantom looked up, and, as he expected, saw small globes of light, weaving and drifting in the air about twenty feet overhead.

The Phantom was about to grab one of them by the shoulder, when the front door of the Dart house was kicked open and a woman strode out to the edge of the porch.

"Just what in the *hell* is all this?" she said, raising a shotgun to her shoulder. "I have had about enough bullshit."

She aimed the shotgun at one of the strange marauders and fired. The blast knocked the man backward onto the lawn. The Phantom dashed over to have a look at the prone figure, and noticed with some relief that the shotgun had been loaded with rock salt rather than buckshot. The sound of the shot had thrown the other stalkers into a mild state of confusion. Some of them had come to a halt, while others moved about in small circles, as though trying to reorient themselves.

Shorty and Louis stepped back toward the street with their hands raised.

"We ain't with these birds, lady." Louis said. "We're here to help you."

"I can see that," the woman said, racking the shotgun again. "But it looks like you're the ones that need help." She drew a bead on another of the shambling figures and squeezed the trigger. The man went down on the lawn and remained there.

At that point, as though obeying a secret command, the rest of the shamblers turned toward the street and began to plod away from the house, going in different directions when they reached the street.

"Should we go after 'em, Boss?" Louis asked nervously.

"No. They won't lead us anywhere. We stay here and look after Mrs. Dart."

"Yes, right, that's good," Louis said brightly, very much relieved.

The Phantom examined the two men who had been felled by Maizie's shotgun blasts. They were alive, but unconscious. The Phantom directed Shorty and Louis to put them into the back seat of Shorty's car.

"Take them to this address," he said, giving them a card. "It's across the Bay, a small clinic I have an interest in. Ask for either Doctor Atticus or Doctor Finch. I doubt Atticus will be there now. Finch most certainly will. Tell him I sent you and that you have two more men in the same condition as the one Doctor Atticus brought in recently."

Maizie Dart tended to strike people as somewhat dull-witted, but she wasn't. She never spoke unless she had something worth saying, and generally expressed thoughts that seemed at odds with *conventional wisdom*—a term often applied to popular foolishness. Her views on religion, politics, and social issues were, she believed, best left unshared with most of the people around her.

She didn't know quite what to make of this masked man and his friends, though she had an idea who he was. She watched him come up the walk after his men had driven off.

"Good evening, Mrs. Dart," he said politely, tipping his hat. "You and I need to have a serious talk."

"You're that guy," she said. "The Bay Phantom. Tom has mentioned you before. He works with you, doesn't he?" She made it sound like a mild accusation.

"We... have an arrangement," the Phantom allowed.

She gave him a thin, rather sad smile. "I thought so. He never said as much, but I knew he had some kind of something going on. And I knew he didn't trust very many people he worked with. Well, he was right about *that*, wasn't he?"

"Very much so, yes."

"And maybe he was right about you. Maybe. Where were you while he was being railroaded?"

"Working to derail it, but in vain. He has some very powerful enemies, Mrs. Dart. But I *will* prevent his execution—one way or another."

She studied him for a few long moments, then slowly nodded her head.

"Yes," she said, "I believe you will. I don't usually trust anonymous men in masks, but the conviction in your voice would be difficult to fake.

Unless you're totally crazy. But that wouldn't necessarily be a liability when you're talking about breaking a man out of Death Row. That *is* what you're talking about, right?"

"I won't lie to you; it will most likely come to that. All possible legal remedies have been exhausted. There will be no more appeals. You certainly know all of this. And time will soon run out."

"Well," she said, "come on inside. I need to check on my daughter anyhow. And if you're thinking of trying anything, I still have one more load of rock salt in this gun."

"Yes, ma'am," said the Phantom.

In the middle of the living room stood a little girl clad in pajamas, rubbing one eye with a fist.

"Mommy, I thought I heard thunder." She saw the strange man who had accompanied her mother into the house. "Hey, Mister, what are you?"

The Phantom knelt down in front of her—Maizie keeping an eye on him, and also keeping a grip on her shotgun—and said, "I am called the Bay Phantom. You must be Coral. Tom has spoken of you to me. He said you were a very pretty little girl, and I can see that he was telling the truth. It's very nice to meet you."

"You know my Daddy?"

"Yes, he and I are friends."

"My Daddy's in jail."

"I know. That's what I've come to speak to your mother about. I hope I can help free him and bring him back to you."

"That would be nice."

"Okay," Maizie said, taking Coral by one hand. "You've had enough excitement. Back to bed you go."

"How come you got a gun?"

"Never mind, let's go."

After she got Coral tucked back into bed, Maizie rejoined the Phantom in the living room.

"I won't get my hopes up too high," she said. "But, I'll be honest with you; I never quite let them go entirely flat. I just had this feeling. I get those sometimes. I didn't know it was about *you*, but I've been expecting something. So, the mysterious Bay Phantom is to be our salvation. Okay, when do we get started?"

"As soon as we can."

"And what are we going to do?"

"For a start, I'd like you to come with me, you and Coral. I can keep you safe until we free Tom and clear up this—whatever is going on."

"I'm supposed to leave everything behind and trust myself and my little girl to a masked man I don't know from Adam?"

"Basically, yes," the Phantom acknowledged.

Maizie bit her lip and studied the Phantom as though he were a pill that might give her immortality, or might kill her instantly if she swallowed it. Finally, she shrugged. "Okay. What the hell. I don't have anything else going on. You know, I've had trouble before tonight. That's why I have the gun. We've had a couple of attempted break-ins. I ran them off. Put some rock salt into their behinds."

"Really? What do you think they might have been after?"

"Not the silverware. I think it was someone from the police force, wanting to see if Tom had left anything behind that might have hinted at his frame-up."

The Phantom nodded.

"There's nothing like that here," Maizie continued. "I would know. We're dealing with some sick people. The whole department is corrupt. Except maybe Carl Matranga. *Maybe* him."

The Phantom nodded. "You can stay with my friend, Joe Perrone," he said.

"Your friend," Maizie repeated.

"Yes. I've known him for a long time, and he's been quite a help to me. He lives in a rather secluded house, with plenty of amenities, and you'll be quite safe there while we arrange for Tom's release."

"Well, Tom trusts you, and I guess that's good enough for me. They've been saying you were involved in some killings, but that's the same thing they did with Tom."

Maizie packed a few small suitcases for herself and Coral. The Phantom loaded them into the trunk of his car. Maizie locked up the house and they were ready to go.

Maizie carried Coral out to the car. The little girl was sound asleep, and she made a little pallet of blankets in the back seat.

"You know," she said as the Phantom put the sedan in gear, "Tom warned me before we got married that being a cop's wife might be difficult. But, I mean, *damn*."

The Phantom cleared his throat.

"Tom's wife and daughter should stay here with us," The Phantom said when he got back to Tull House. He had left Maizie and Coral in the car while he went in to brief Mirabelle. "It's the best way to ensure their safety."

"I guess you're right," Mirabelle said. "And since you already brought them here..."

"You say your plan to rescue Tom is ready to go. We need to get on that, and it will be best if his family is in a place where we can look after them. They're out in the car now. If you wouldn't mind seeing to them, I'd appreciate it. I told them Joe Perrone is a friend of mine, and I suppose he should make an appearance. I'll drive the sedan away, then down into the underground garage. Put the Darts up in the South Room. I'll be along directly."

The Phantom brought Maizie and Coral in from the car, introduced them to Mirabelle, then took his leave. Mirabelle explained that she often did favors for the Phantom, as did her boss, Joe Perrone, who was busy doing something or other and would make an appearance soon. In the meantime, she escorted them up to the South Room and helped them stow their belongings.

"Okay," Mirabelle said when everything was squared away and the Phantom had taken his leave, "are either of you hungry? Because I could use something to eat."

"Me, me!" Coral exclaimed. "I'm staaaarrrving!"

"Coral!" Maizie said. "Mind your manners!"

"Oh, that's all right," Mirabelle said. "Nobody in this house has any manners. Let's go down to the kitchen and see what we can find."

While they were eating chicken sandwiches, Joe Perrone came up from the cellar to meet his new guests.

Mirabelle gave Maizie a very rough outline of her plan to save Tom. She left out most of the details, not wanting to drive the poor woman into a panic.

"We need you to write him a letter," Mirabelle explained. "I'll write the text out for you, and you can copy it in your own handwriting."

"You have a plan to get him out," Maizie said with no inflection.

"I do," Mirabelle confirmed. "It's risky, but I believe with all my heart that it will work. I'm asking you to trust me. What I give you to copy out will let Tom know that we have it covered, and a bit of what to expect."

After Maizie and Coral went to bed, Perrone and Mirabelle sat down in the living room to discuss the events of the evening.

"It's interesting how those blasts of rock salt put those men down when my anesthetic gas had no effect on them," Perrone said at one point.

"That *is* curious," Mirabelle agreed. "You know, salt has a lot of occult significance."

"I've heard that. I wish Charles Fort were still alive, I'd like to ask him about it."

"Well, you know, my daddy was a sort of houngan, and I remember some things. I know that salt was the one substance that could deactivate a zombie."

Perrone had winced slightly at the mention of Mirabelle's father, but she hadn't noticed.

"Do you think that's what they are?" he asked. "Zombies?"

"Of course not, don't be asinine."

"Doctor Atticus hasn't been able to discover anything from the, ah, gentleman I introduced to him."

"Yeah... If Ambrose can't figure it out..." She shook her head. "No. No, there's an answer, and it's not Voodoo."

"Well, perhaps Atticus will discover something from these latest two."

"Yeah, perhaps."

CHAPTER FIFTEEN
WINONA'S DREAMS

Winona had been having dreams. They made no sense at all from a waking point of view, but while she was in them, they had a certain confusing logic.

In the dreams, she was dead and she knew it. She walked in a gray and misty place that was both death and life, and she was being allowed to do this for reasons she didn't quite understand. She needed to accomplish something, not for herself, but for someone else.

Time didn't seem to have much meaning here, but there was a sense of urgency.

She saw a great Beast who straddled the line between life and death. It was huge and dark, with tentacles and great staring eyes. This creature was surrounded by small figures, walking dead men who were somehow in thrall to the Beast, controlled by it. They turned their dead eyes to Winona and they spoke with one voice:

"Who is like unto the beast? Who is able to make war with him?"

She knew the answer to their questions, but she was afraid to say it. The front of her body was slit down the middle. She reached inside for something to fight with, but there was nothing there.

She wasn't alone, though. Another woman was there with her, the strangest-looking woman Winona had ever seen. She wore a gown of some sort with peculiar designs embroidered all over it in gold thread, and her face was a white, dead mask. Winona knew that whatever she was lacking, this woman possessed, and vice versa.

And there was a boy. She never saw him, but she knew he was there. He was an unwitting agent of order, masquerading as pure, blind chance. He had no idea of his own true nature.

CHAPTER SIXTEEN

INSIDE MAN

Just before ten o'clock on the night after he brought Tom Dart's family to Tull House, the Bay Phantom went on a solo mission. He used the tunnel that led from Tull House to the Church Street Grave Yard, employing the small railway and sidecar that had been installed under the ground a couple of years previously.

After taking the short journey on his little railcar, the Phantom emerged from a mock grave on Church Street, carefully securing the entrance, which was disguised to look like a hundred-year-old stone slab.

The little cemetery was six blocks from police headquarters, and he covered the distance on foot, keeping to the shadows, cutting through yards and across roofs.

From across the street, he observed a single lighted window on the second floor. That was where he would find the man he had come to see.

Moving around to the rear of the building, he tossed a stout line with a grappling hook onto the roof and silently ascended.

This was not the first time the Phantom had gained entry to the building via the roof, and he knew just where to go. There was a small trapdoor in the middle of the roof that had not been discovered by anyone in the two years it had existed. The Phantom himself had installed it one spring afternoon, in the guise of a city maintenance worker.

Once inside, he glided silently through the empty halls of the third floor and on down the stairs at the rear of the building. He crept along the second floor hallway until he came to a door. Light shone through the pebbled glass in the upper panel. Small letters on the lower right side of the pane said, "Detective Lieutenant Carl Matranga." The Phantom gently gripped the knob, turned it soundlessly, pushed the door open, and stepped in, quickly shutting it behind him.

"Good evening, Lieutenant Matranga," he said affably. "I thought I might find you here, even at this hour. You have a reputation for diligence."

"Well," Matranga said, putting his pen down on his desk and leaning back in his chair. He seemed unusually calm, as though this intrusion were not particularly unexpected—or unwelcome. "I don't reckon I need to ask who you are. You're a wanted man, you know. How'd you get in here?"

"Breaking and entering, technically, though I caused no damage. You could arrest me, Lieutenant, but I would be obliged to resist, and I am more than capable of doing so successfully."

"Oh, I don't doubt that. I've seen you at work. So, what can I do for you?"

"I was hoping you and I could have a little chat," said the masked man.

"About?"

"A few things. The recent murders, for one. Tom Dart, for another. Oh, and Eliot Ness."

"I see. And why should I talk to you about any of those things? You gonna rough me up if I don't? I mean, I've got a gun, but from what I've heard about you, you could take it off me before I had a chance to use it, so..."

The Phantom shook his head and held up his hands.

"No, no, nothing like that. If you don't wish to talk with me, I'll leave. However—from what *I've* heard about *you*, you're a decent man, and I think you and I might have similar points of view. Particularly about poor Tom. If you're not interested, I'll wish you a pleasant evening and be on my way."

"Goddamn, you sure are polite. Well, hell, sit down. Lemme hear what's on your mind."

The Phantom nodded and pulled a wooden chair that was against the wall closer to Matranga's desk and seated himself. The masked man had decided to waste no time on rigmarole or pleasantries; it was time for the direct approach.

"Are you being pressured?" the Phantom asked. "That is to say, do you find your efforts at honest police work stymied by those above you in the department?"

Matranga cleared his throat and squirmed a little in his chair. "Well, I don't know that I—I mean, why should I tell you anything?"

"I don't expect you to confide in me," the Phantom said, in a voice almost completely free of inflection. "But I think you answered my question just the same. Let us take it as a working hypothesis, for the sake of this conversation, that you are. You may or may not know or suspect where this pressure is coming from. I would be surprised if you had not indulged in some conjecture. I believe that a group of individuals, highly placed in the government of this city, have for some time been involved in a conspiracy of corruption. I believe that may be why the federal government has taken an interest."

"Yeah, Eliot Ness. He approached me, you know. How he picked me out, I don't know, but he gave me basically the same line you're giving. He thinks I can be trusted. I—haven't said anything to him one way or the other, though."

"Obviously, you have a reputation."

"Jesus, I hope not. I don't like corruption, but I like breathing. I know Tom suspected something about the city government, and the police force, probably a lot of things. He never confided in me, but he made remarks now and then. And look what happened to him! I've got a family to feed."

"So does Tom," the Phantom replied softly. There was no note of judgment in his voice, but Matranga didn't need it to feel guilty.

"What about those guys you set on fire? That was pretty harsh."

"I didn't do that. You've been in Mobile longer than I have, and you ought to be familiar with my activities. When have I ever been known to set anyone on fire?"

"You do have a point there. But, hell, I don't know what to believe any more—about *anybody*."

This was the moment, the Phantom sensed. Matranga was dying to talk to someone about something. The railroading of Tom Dart, for one thing. And who knew what else the man was privy to but felt powerless to do anything about?

"Here's the thing," Matranga said. "Maybe I know about some stuff. Not much, but some. *Maybe*. And *maybe* there have been some things going on that I don't like. *Maybe* my superiors are keeping tight control of what goes on around here, what gets investigated and what doesn't, and who

"Maybe I know about some stuff."

gets to know about things. And *maybe*, Mister Phantom, more than just my job is it stake if I make any waves, even little ones. Do you get what I'm saying?"

The Phantom nodded. "Yes, and I think I get even more from what you're *not* saying."

"I imagine you do. And my problem right now is this: I've got a man in a mask sitting in my office and he claims to be the Bay Phantom. Anybody can put on a mask. One of Chief Prater's boys, or maybe even Prater himself, could get done up to look like the Bay Phantom and come in here to see what I might or might not spill. You see where I'm coming from?"

"I do indeed. I have no identification I can offer you. I could remove my mask, but you don't know who I am, you've probably never seen me before. I could be a hireling of Chief Prater's or someone else's. But here's something that occurs to me: Without giving any details, you have still revealed enough about your attitude to land you in hot water with your superiors if I'm a spy. You could at least be fired for what you have said, if not disposed of more definitively. So why did you say what you said to me just now?"

The Phantom could tell that the question had taken Matranga unawares; the man did not know the answer! But the Phantom was sure that he did. Matranga was desperate, miserable, cornered, and he needed to have some small glimmer of faith in *something*.

If that something was a hat, a cloak, a mask, and a pair of goggles, then so be it.

The Phantom drew breath to speak, to offer a sympathetic ear to the troubled policeman.

Several sharp cracks sounded from the floor below. Gunshots. Then there was a loud boom and a rumble and the whole building shuddered.

"What the shit!" Matranga shouted, leaping to his feet.

"Good heavens!" the Phantom exclaimed, springing lithely from his chair.

They dashed through the door of the office, down the hall, to the stairs.

On the ground floor, they were met with a horrific sight.

Several police officers lay scattered about the hallway. Two of them were obviously dead, their heads shattered. The others were grievously injured at the very least. A few were grappling with the by now all-too-familiar shambling men.

A few of the queer "fireflies" had entered the building as well, but they did not seem to be playing any part in the conflicts. It was as though their function was simply to monitor—or perhaps control—the shambling men.

Smoke hung in the air. Somewhere, an alarm blared. But anyone nearby who might answer it lay scattered about the hallway, unable to respond.

"Down there at the end of the hall," Matranga said. "It's the holding cell where that character from Chicago is."

Through the smoke, they could see that the holding cell had been blasted open. The door lay on the floor, twisted and smoldering.

Jack Foregone was dragging the Mouse out of the cell. The little man seemed stunned, but unhurt.

Forgone must have shot his way into the building and used a bomb or a grenade to crack open the cell. The explosion had ripped through the hallway. Those officers who had not been immediately subdued found themselves harried by the shambling men.

"Let's go, Mouse," Foregone was saying. "Get it together. Kraken's waiting for us."

The Mouse nodded. "Yeah, Jack, I'm okay, let's go."

"I've had about enough of you fellows," the Phantom said, stepping forward through the smoke, automatics drawn. "You have no regard for human life at all."

"Oh, it's the masked man again!" Forgone said. "You're right, we really don't. But let me show you something, pal. See that guard over there?" He pointed to a uniformed man propped up against the wall next to the ruined cell. The man had something strapped to his chest. It was quite obvious to the Phantom what that something was. "He ain't dead, not yet. But you'll notice that little contraption on him. That's a time bomb, and it's got about a minute to go, maybe less, I dunno. Now, to show you how much regard I've got for human life, I'm gonna give you a choice. You can come after us, or you can save him. That bomb's easy to dismantle, but it'll take a little time. Up to you, masked man."

"I can stop you," Matranga said, charging toward Foregone, while the Phantom moved to the man against the wall.

The Scarecrow let go of the Mouse and darted forward, swatting Matranga's gun hand, causing his shot to go into the floor, and punching the cop hard in the face, knocking him to the ground. Then he whirled back around, grabbed the Mouse by the arm, and pulled him up the hallway toward the front door.

While this was going on, the Phantom disabled the explosive device, a very simple job—just an alarm clock, some wires, and a single stick of dynamite—then went to Matranga, who was sitting up, pressing his necktie to his nose to stop the flow of blood.

The shambling men had ceased to move. The all stood stock-still, as though they knew their part in the proceedings was over, and they had no further purpose. The "fireflies" had vanished.

"Are you all right, Lieutenant?" the masked man asked.

"Shit, no, I ain't all right," Matranga grumbled. "They're gone. Ness warned me he might try something. That's why I had extra guards down here. I just set them up to die."

"You weren't expecting an attack like this," the Phantom said sympathetically. "You couldn't have prepared for it. Anyone who would think of attaching that bomb to a wounded man has a mind too sick and devious to anticipate."

Matranga said nothing.

"I'll find them, Lieutenant," the Phantom added. "I promise you that."

Matranga nodded. "Do that. And if they don't make it to trial, I won't complain. Just give me something to prove they're—you know."

"I'll bring them in alive, if possible."

"If it ain't possible, don't sweat it. Now you better beat it before someone else gets here."

The Phantom nodded and glided off into the smoke.

"Jesus," Matranga said. "Sweet Jesus Christ, what have I gotten into?"

The Phantom left the building by a rear door. He found no trace of the Scarecrow and the Mouse. Keeping to the shadows, he made his way back to the Church Street Grave Yard and his secret tunnel.

CHAPTER SEVENTEEN

TRUST

The day following the attack on police headquarters, things were more or less back to normal. The rubble had been cleared away, and repairs had begun. The damage to the building, apart from the holding cell that had been blown open, was minimal. The loss of life hadn't been as bad as it could have been, but that wasn't much consolation. In the days ahead, there would be three police funerals.

Matranga was in his office, working on his report on the incident—a report which omitted any mention of the Bay Phantom.

There wasn't too much to tell. Armed with a pair of automatics, Jack Foregone had shot his way into the building, accompanied by a cadre of the shambling men, and then lobbed a hand grenade at the holding cell door, after shouting a warning to the Mouse. The guards and other officers on duty had been taken completely by surprise. A couple of them had managed to get off some shots at the invaders, but Foregone had evidently been wearing a bullet-proof vest.

All of the shambling men had been hit by gunfire; two of them had been killed. The ten who were left alive had numerous bullet holes in non-vital spots. They had ignored these injuries and continued what they were doing until they had "deactivated."

Matranga shook his head. What did it mean? What the *hell* was going on?

There was a knock at the door. Matranga said, "Come in."

Eliot Ness stepped into the office.

"Don't tell me you told me so," Matranga said ruefully.

"I wouldn't," Ness said. "I hate people who do that. I'm a little surprised Foregone took it as far as he did. He seems to be evolving, and not in a good way."

"There's something funny going on in this town," Matranga said. "And I don't mean *that* in a good way."

"Anything new on the killings?"

Matranga set his report aside and picked up a sheet of yellow legal paper on which he had made some notes earlier in the day.

"What I've learned," he said, "is that the guys who are still locked up down there for those killings—as well as a number of the ones from the other night—were regulars at the St. Dymphna Rescue Mission downtown. I'll bet the same is true of the ones that Foregone left behind when he sprung his boyfriend. There's gotta be some kind of connection."

"You sent anybody down there?" Ness asked.

Matranga shook his head. "The Chief won't allow it. 'A waste of department resources,' he says. We got the guys, and that's all there is to it."

"The Chief says," Ness added.

"Yeah," Matranga said. "He doesn't seem to care about finding any explanation for why they were doing what they were doing."

"You know," Ness said, "I see what's going on in this town. I've talked to you about this before. I'm not going to insult your intelligence by trying to tell you that you can trust me, because I know what it's like to be in a situation where you don't know who you can trust. I've been there before, and I'll probably be there again. But you know who I am and what I've done. And if there's anything that's bugging you about what's going on in this town, and you want to say anything about it, it won't go any farther than just between you and me."

Matranga looked at him, really *looked* at him. He was trying to make a decision, or maybe trying not to, but Ness knew he'd hit some kind of a vein.

Ness was sure Matranga was as clean and honest a cop as could be found in this town. And he was equally sure that any progress Matranga made toward the truth would be blocked from above. Something was going on here. He'd seen it in Chicago. A few good cops were kept on the payroll to keep up appearances, but they were never allowed to advance, they were constantly frustrated by their superiors. They knew exactly what was going on, but they felt powerless. So they just bided their time, hoping their day would come.

"Unless you *want* it to," Ness added. "I'm going to be straight with you. I never came to Mobile after that goddamn Werewolf. That was a blind. You probably guessed as much. I came here because this city is corrupt from the top down, and I know you know that too. But specifically, I came here because of the Scarecrow and the Mouse. See, we had a wiretap on one of the Capone safe houses where they were staying, and over the past few months, they had multiple phone contacts with public officials here in Mobile. After it became clear Capone was finished, they vanished. We couldn't turn them up in any of their usual haunts, and we finally decided they might have come here, seeking new employment. It looks like we were right."

Matranga's lips had compressed into a very thin line while Ness had spoken. "The sons of bitches," he said coldly. It wasn't clear who he was referring to, but Ness had some ideas.

He placed a hand on Matranga's shoulder.

"We'll get 'em, Carl," he promised.

Matranga looked him in the eye for a long while. Then he nodded.

"So," Ness went on, "what does the Chief say about this attack on headquarters, and the Mouse getting sprung?"

"Officially, he's lying about it. The story that's going out is that a gas main exploded. Me and the rest of the guys who were here when it happened have been told in no uncertain terms that we're not to talk to the press or to anybody else. If anyone is doing an actual investigation, I haven't been let in on it."

"What about me?"

Matranga smiled. "Dang, I wasn't supposed to tell *you*, either. And look what I've done now, I let it slip. Me and my big mouth."

Ness smiled back. "Damn careless of you, Lieutenant. Any other interesting, ah, *anomalies* you might accidentally let slip?"

Neither of them knew that the janitor, Chester, was in the hallway outside the door, wiping the baseboard, and memorizing every word he heard them say.

"We found two lumps of *something* lying on the ground between the bodies," Matranga told Ness. "Some kind of metal or something. It looks kinda like lead, but it's got a little greenish tint to it, or yellowish, depending on how the light strikes it."

"What? Can I see it?"

Matranga shrugged. "Sure, if you'd like. It's in the evidence room. Come on."

The left the office, brushing past Chester, and went downstairs. Neither man noticed the janitor as he trailed along behind them.

Matranga unlocked the evidence room and he and Ness stepped inside. From a cardboard carton, the detective lifted a lump of metal wrapped in newspaper. He unwrapped the thing and handed it to Ness. The federal agent examined it, turning it this way and that under a bare lightbulb.

"Matranga," said Ness, "this is *uranium*."

"Whaaat?"

Ness nodded. "Yep. I'm sure of it. I've seen the stuff before."

"Is it dangerous?" Matranga asked, shrinking back a bit.

"Not really, so long as you don't eat it." Ness turned the chunk over in his hands. "What in the hell is it doing *here*?"

Something clicked in his head and he felt a chill. "There's a connection between this stuff and what was written on the walls at the scenes of those murders. Einstein's formula, E=MC2; energy equals mass times the velocity of light squared."

"What does that mean, exactly?"

"I don't know, it's over my head. But it has to do with matter and energy, and here we have some matter that's radioactive—it produces energy."

"What could it mean?" Matranga wondered.

"I don't know, but I do know one thing: A couple of burned-out rummies weren't going around with chunks of a rare metal, cutting people open and writing an esoteric scientific formula on walls in their blood."

"Yeah, I got that much already. But who *did* do it? And *why*?"

Ness shook his head. "That, I can't even imagine."

CHAPTER EIGHTEEN

THE GUARD

Keys clattered in the lock and Tom Dart's cell door swung open. Tom looked up to see one of the guards, Dale Sander, a man whose physical appearance matched his temper: short and ugly.

"Hey," he said. "How are you and your little nigger boyfriend next door getting along down here? Sorry we ain't got the heat on today, but there's a nice warm chair down at the end of the hall waiting on you boys. Won't be too much longer now. Anyhow, I got some mail for you. From your old lady, I guess." He held up a lavender-colored envelope.

He tossed the envelope in Tom's direction, deliberately letting it fall to the floor a few feet short of the prisoner. Tom got to his feet, advanced a few steps, and stooped to pick it up.

Sander advanced a couple of steps and kicked Tom on the side of the head, not very hard, more contemptuous than aggressive.

Tom crouched there on the cold floor, head hanging, his fingers resting on the envelope. Sander stood over him, smirking.

They were still for a couple of seconds, then Tom abruptly sprang to his feet, smacking Sander in the jaw with the top of his head. The guard slammed into the wall and fumbled for his pistol, blood streaming from the corners of his mouth. He got his weapon clear, and Tom snatched it out of his grip, tossing it to the rear of the cell. He slammed the door with his foot and caught Sander by the throat, pressing him back up against the wall.

"You listen to me, you little worm," Tom said, his lips just an inch or two from the guard's ear. "Fact is, I could kill you right now, and you know it. Fact is, I could kill you any time I want, that's how sorry you are. Fact is, I'm just a better man than you'll ever be—and that so-called 'nigger' over there is too. And, you know? They can't electrocute me but once. If I was to finish you off right now, there'd have to be another trial, and that'd buy me at least six more months of life. Sounds like kind of a good idea, now that I think of it. Don't you think so?"

Sander glared back at him.

Tom tightened his grip on the man's throat.

"I asked you don't you think it's a good idea?"

The hate in Sander's eyes gave way to fear. He shook his head.

"What?" Tom whispered. "You don't?"

Sander shook his head as emphatically as he could with Tom's hand around his throat.

"All right," Tom said, letting him go. "Pick up your gun and get the hell out of my cell. And stay out of my way, or so help me God, I will crack your skull open if it's the last thing I do on this earth."

Avoiding Tom's gaze, Sander retrieved his pistol and slunk out of the cell, locking the door behind him.

"Hey, cop," came the voice of Lucas Horne a minute later. "You okay, man. You crazy as hell, but you okay. I think I'm gonna miss you."

Tom sat down on his bunk and sat for a few moments gazing at the envelope. It was from Maizie all right. The sight of her handwriting both calmed him and filled him with deep sorrow. He tore it open and pulled out two sheets of paper, quickly reading them.

It only took him a few seconds to realize what he was looking at. The letter had been written by Maizie, no doubt about that, but parts of the message seemed to ramble and made little sense. That was because they were in a code that had been taught to him by the Bay Phantom. This in itself came as a relief to him. It meant that Maizie and Coral were safe; the Phantom wouldn't let anything happen to them.

He read the message. For the first time in months, he smiled.

CHAPTER NINETEEN
THE MISSION

"About Maizie," Mirabelle said. "She isn't stupid."

They were back at the kitchen table, two days after Maizie and Coral had come to Tull House. Mirabelle had a tumbler of wine. Perrone had looked askance at it and said something about it being rather early in the day, but Mirabelle had ignored him.

"I agree with that," Perrone replied cautiously, wondering where Mirabelle was headed.

"She's not dull," Mirabelle went on. "She's not typical. When she looks at me, she doesn't just see some nigger girl that works for someone, she sees another human being."

"That's good, yes?" Perrone had winced at the racial slur, though he ought to have been used to hearing Mirabelle toss it around by now. Something akin to gallows humor, he supposed, and he had stopped remarking on it. He hoped she would break herself of the habit one day, but knew that if she did it simply for his sake, it wouldn't be any good. It was just the world they lived in, after all. Even among his very limited circle of acquaintances, he heard that word spoken—without any irony—four or five times a week.

"Yes, it is," she said, "but it's also problematic. From a Bay Phantom standpoint, I mean."

"Yes. Well, I suppose we'll just have to trust her. I mean, there's really nothing else for it, is there?"

"Right. But she's going to know that our association with the Bay Phantom is closer than we have intimated. She probably does already."

"I know," said Perrone. "But her well-being, and Coral's, are more important than any of my petty secrets. You continue with your preparations, and continue to reassure Maizie."

"What are *you* going to be doing?"

"I want to have a look at that rescue mission. I have a feeling some answers might be found there. These murders and the situation at City Hall tie into Tom's troubles. I want to see if I can learn anything tonight."

"Well, be careful, I'm gonna need you in good shape."

"Don't worry, I'm taking Louis with me."

"Oh, Jesus."

The Phantom had sent Shorty Red to Chicago, to turn up any information he could on Jack Foregone and Mark Mills. Anything that might suggest why they had come South; any connections they might have had to anybody in Mobile. Shorty could be trusted with such a mission.

Louis Rickert was another story. Louis had potential, the Phantom believed, but he needed to be supervised at all times.

Driving his sedan, he picked Louis up at a prearranged rendezvous point, and proceeded from there to Water Street.

“There it is,” he said as they cruised past the place. “The St. Dymphna Rescue Mission.” The square, two-story, whitewashed building stood between a warehouse and a vacant lot. A group of shabbily-dressed men milled around on the sidewalk outside.

The Phantom drove past and parked the car two blocks north, close to the old train terminal.

“This is to be a stealth operation, Louis,” he said in a slightly pedantic tone. “That means we avoid any confrontations with anybody.”

“That suits me fine, Boss. I’ve had enough confrontations to last me ’til Christmas.”

“I’m going to remove my mask now, but I must tell you that the face you see will not be my own. I have made myself up, and will do the same for you.” The Phantom took off his goggles and rolled the black mask up and away, taking care not to disarrange the makeup that lay beneath.

Louis gawked at the face that was revealed. He found himself sharing the front seat of the Phantom’s sedan with a bleary, bewhiskered man in his late 60s, with thinning hair, sunken cheeks, and rheumy eyes.

“Oh,” Louis said, “we’re gonna pass ourselves off as a couple of bums, then.”

“A couple of men in unfortunate circumstances, if you please,” the Phantom primly corrected him. “That is why I asked you not to shave and to wear a disreputable suit. I see you chose to ignore the latter request.”

“What?” Louis said indignantly. “I wore the best suit I have.”

“I can see that. I suppose I should have clarified the meaning of *disreputable*. Well, no matter, just remove your tie, disarrange your shirt and hair, and crumple your hat a bit. I’ll buy you a new one later.”

Grumbling a bit, Louis complied. He and the Phantom stepped out of the car. As they walked back toward the mission, Louis studied his companion in the light from a street lamp.

“Hey,” he said, “that’s a nice bum suit you’ve got there, Boss. Say, you ain’t been putting on weight, have you?”

In fact, the crime fighter was wearing his specially-designed Bay Phantom suit underneath the shabby clothing. One never knew what one might run into, and he might need some of the gadgets that were stored in the concealed pockets. The “bum suit” was actually very lightweight. The fact that he had another suit on underneath was not apparent, but the extra clothing did give him a bulkier appearance, which was helpful in terms of disguise.

“Never mind, Louis. Just get into character. Remember, you are a poor, unfortunate man who has seen better days, and has fallen on evil times through no fault of your own."

"Sure, got it."

"Here we are," the Phantom whispered as they reached the front of the mission. A line of men were assembled on the sidewalk, waiting for the doors to open.

Louis snorted. "Now we gotta stand in line, jeez. I hope we don't have to listen to a bunch of preaching when we get in there."

"Hush, Louis, it might do you some good."

They did not have long to wait. Three minutes after they took their places at the end of the line, a man in black slacks and shirtsleeves pulled open the double doors and waved for the assembled men to come in.

The Phantom and Louis slowly mounted the steps, waiting for those ahead of them to be admitted. Finally, they passed through the doorway.

Just inside the doorway, the man in shirtsleeves sat on a stool behind a tall, narrow desk, with a thick ledger open in front of him. He didn't bother to look up at the new arrivals.

"Need your names," he said, evidently too bored to bother with his own personal pronoun.

"I'm Johnny Dodge," said the Phantom, "and this here's Ted Sims."

"Well, write 'em down on this ledger," he said, thrusting a pen at the Phantom. "I ain't your secretary."

The Phantom signed the ledger with his assumed name, and handed the pen to Louis, watching to make sure he inscribed the correct pseudonym on the page. Then they stepped through the foyer into a large hall. Directly to the right of the inner doorway was a flight of stairs, going up to whatever might be on the second floor

The hall was a typical impersonal gathering place for men with pasts best left unexamined and no futures to speak of. The walls were painted institutional green, with a few hangings here and there: crosses, framed pictures of religious figures, inspirational mottoes.

At the rear of the room was a raised platform with a wooden podium in the center. A photograph of Archbishop Craig hung on the wall behind the podium. The Phantom noticed that the eyes seemed to follow one around the room. Some pictures were like that, it was merely an optical trick.

Most of the main room was taken up by five rows of long tables with mismatched chairs arranged around them. All of the men seated themselves at the tables, and the Phantom and Louis followed suit.

They were subjected to a short sermon delivered by a colorless man who spoke in a monotone of the need for salvation, the necessity of renouncing sin, one variation after another of these sentiments, conveyed in a series of tepid metaphors. It was enough to deaden the spirit of the most ardent churchgoer, and when it was over, all the men in the room were mildly dazed and drained of energy.

Then it was time to eat. Without having to be told, the men rose from their seats and formed a line at the window that opened from the kitchen.

A fellow in an apron handed each man a bowl of soup through the window.

The Phantom ate his, while Louis merely stared down into his bowl with an expression of dismay. As he ate, the Phantom scanned the room with his eyes. Nothing interesting happened for several minutes. Then he saw something: Two men slipped through the foyer and went up the stairs. Jack Forgone and Mark Mills. No one else had noticed them enter.

He kept an eye on the stairway. The Scarecrow and the Mouse came back down less than a minute later. Each of them was carrying a large suitcase.

There was no point in trying to catch up with them. Instead, the Phantom decided to take a look at whatever was upstairs.

He leaned over to his companion.

"Louis," he whispered, "I need you to create a small diversion. Nothing outrageous, just enough to draw everyone's attention while I slip upstairs."

"What should I do, Boss?"

"Pretend to be ill. Act as though you were having a heart attack or something of the sort. All I need is a few minutes."

"Oh, sure. Me and Pete Cable used to do a trick like that. Pete would pretend to have a fit, and I'd lift as many wallets as I could while people were paying attention to him."

"Uh—yes. Same principle. Just let me get to the other side of the room, then proceed."

He picked up his bowl and walked over to the kitchen window to return it. He nodded across the room to Louis, and began sidling along the wall toward the stairs.

"Oh, God!" Louis exclaimed, rising from his chair. "I think I'm having a stroke. I get 'em sometimes." He clutched at his chest. "Aowwww! The pain!"

Every head in the hall turned toward him. He staggered around in a circle, moaning softly like a kitten, then lowered himself gently to the floor, to lay prone. Most of the men rose from their seats and craned their necks.

Several of them came over to gawk down at him. The doorkeeper came into the hall and went to where Louis lay. The Phantom dashed up the stairs.

On the second floor, he found a hallway with two rooms on each side. He tried the door immediately to his right and found himself in what appeared to be an office. He took a quick look around, but saw nothing of interest. There was a desk with nothing on it; a filing cabinet which he quickly discovered had nothing in it (which was odd in itself).

Crouching down in the hallway, he discerned faint footmarks left very recently by two men. The Scarecrow and the Mouse, no doubt. They led directly to and from a door at the end of the hall.

He swiftly picked the lock, and found himself looking into a small storeroom. There were brooms and mops leaned up against the left-hand wall, and a row of shelves along the right. It was there that he made an intriguing discovery.

There were four shelves running along the wall, parallel to one another. The top three held a variety of pedestrian items: cleaning products, a box of envelopes, a few light bulbs in cardboard cartons.

The bottom shelf was empty, but, judging by the pattern of dust, it had very recently held something. And it was the dust itself that caught his attention.

It was grayish-yellow, metallic-looking, not the ordinary sort of dust one would expect to find in a place like this. It seemd to glisten slightly in the light from the hallway.

He scooped some together and deposited it into a small glass tube he took from the breast pocket of his Phantom suit.

Downstairs, Louis continued his performance, observed by the roomful of nonplussed derelicts.

But one of the men was not a derelict at all; he was Eliot Ness. Ness had employed disguises before, back in Chicago, and had a pretty good track record with them. Once, he and another of the Untouchables had decked themselves out as vagrants and managed to hitch a ride on one of Capone's beer trucks. Taking on the persona of a bum, Ness knew, was the best way to render oneself almost invisible just about anywhere in the world.

Whatever might be going on in this peculiar rescue mission, he could linger and observe the "clients" and the personnel to his heart's content.

With no other leads to speak of, it just might pay off eventually, though it hadn't so far. He'd been here a couple of times over the past few days.

He was clean-shaven, but had smeared his lower face with grime and was dressed in a shabby suit and a battered hat.

He didn't know what he might hope to discover here, but that was the thing: One never knew. More than once in his life, Ness had caught a large fish in a seemingly dry well. Back in Chicago, he'd picked up plenty of dirt on Capone by spending time in some pretty unlikely places.

Louis was thrashing around on the floor, clutching at his chest. A small crowd of six or eight men had gathered around him.

"If you got a stroke," one of them said, "it'd be in your head, not your heart."

"Oh," Louis said. "Well, it could be a heart attack, I get those too. Oh, the pain!"

He grabbed at the nearest leg and caught hold of the pants cuff.

"Help me!" he wailed. "I think this is it!"

The man whose pants leg Louis was clutching shook loose from his grip and looked down at him.

"Hey," said Rickey Harvard, "I know you. You're that hood, Louis Rickert. What are you doing down here? Planning on stealing something, I bet! You're just low enough to come down here and steal from poor people, ain't you?"

"Shut up kid, beat it," Louis snarled. "My name's Joe Sims or something. I'm just here for some soup, and now I'm dying."

"You can't fool me. You been bugging me for a while now. You stole one of my pictures, didn't you? The one of the redhead? Hey, I oughtta call a cop is what I oughtta do!"

Several men looked around nervously at the mention of the police.

"This guy's a crook!" Rickey said, jabbing a finger at Louis. "You all better watch out he don't pick your pockets!"

Several men stepped up to have a closer look at Louis.

"Look at that suit," one of them said. "It musta cost at least forty bucks. That kid's right, he's up to something."

"That kid's crazy," Louis wailed, "I ain't no crook!"

"Naw," said another of the men, "I recognize you. You and Pete Cable used to pull this shit alla time in Bienville Square! You think you gonna come down here and steal from *us* now?" The man looked around the room. "He's got a partner somewhere. Let's get these bums."

The whole room erupted at that point. Men turned on one another.

Old grudges and new suspicions inflamed the crowd. A few blows were exchanged, then more. Several of the men converged on Louis.

Ness tried to get through the chaos to the center of the ruckus. Failing that, he skirted the edge of the flailing crowd and ran outside to a payphone on the corner to call the police emergency line. The whole thing needed to be stopped before somebody in there got killed.

The Phantom was carefully locking the storeroom door when he heard the banging and raised voices from downstairs. Shaking his head sadly, he stripped off the camouflage outfit. Removing his cloak from a pouch sewn into the back of the Bay Phantom jacket, he stuffed the "bum suit" into the pouch, donned his mask and goggles, replaced his hat and jacket, and fastened the cloak around his shoulders.

Now the "Johnny Dodge" identity could be preserved, in case he might be needed again.

All of this took only a handful of seconds, and then the Phantom was ready to descend into whatever maelstrom Louis had created. He took the steps two at a time.

Louis had taken advantage of the general chaos to avoid the men who had been intent on getting their hands on him. He had stayed close to the ground, crawling between flailing legs, worming his way toward the doors. He had just managed to get clear of the brawl and was heading out, when the Phantom reached the bottom of the stairs.

"Oh, for Heaven's sake," the masked man grumbled, snatching Louis by the collar and dragging him toward the door. "I can't leave you alone for five minutes."

"It wasn't my fault, Boss," Louis whispered.

"I know it wasn't," the Phantom replied tersely. "It never is, is it, Louis?"

When they hit the sidewalk they could hear sirens, very close by.

"Jesus," Louis said, "the cops'll be swarming all over the place in a second."

"And they're coming from the north. Well, we'll leave the car and walk back to your place. Just keep to the shadows with me, we'll be fine."

They did not notice the "derelict" who had been standing by the public phone near the mission, and was now trailing them. They traversed the six blocks to the apartment on Dauphin Street where Louis and Shorty were now living, having moved their quarters after the debacle with the shambling men.

As he trailed the pair, the fastidious Ness cleaned his face with a handkerchief, popped the dents out of his hat, and put his tie on.

CHAPTER TWENTY
THE SUIT

"I'll just leave by the window, Louis," said the Phantom, once they had reached the sanctuary of the apartment. "I'll have to walk a few blocks, so it's best I not have this with me. If I should get picked up, there's nothing to connect me to the Bay Phantom. Just hang onto the Phantom suit, would you?" He had removed the Phantom suit and was once more the disheveled derelict.

"What am I supposed to do with it?"

"Nothing. Just keep it for me."

The Phantom opened the window at the rear of the room, the one that overlooked the alleyway, and slipped through, going up instead of down. Louis wondered how he did that. He was about to shut the window again, when someone started banging on his door.

"Federal agent!" came a strident voice from the hallway. "Open up!"

Louis jerked as though he'd been electrocuted. Would this horrible night never end?

"Come on, Rickert, open up! Don't make me get a warrant!"

"Hell, hell, hell," Louis muttered, looking around the little room for a hiding place.

In a moment of near-lucidity, the whole scene reminded him of a Laurel and Hardy picture he'd seen not long ago. Their landlord had been banging on the door and they'd been trying to hide something from him, and *what had they done*?

Oh, yeah!

He bundled up the stuff and tossed it out the window, into the alley below. Then he pulled the window shut and went to the door.

The banging had continued. Louis yelled, "All right, jeez, keep your shirt on, I'm coming!"

He pulled the door open. In the hallway stood a man who looked familiar to Louis. The guy looked a little bit like Jimmy Cagney, but that couldn't be who it was. It was somebody famous, though. Louis was sure he'd seen that face somewhere.

Then it dawned on him. It was Eliot Ness! He'd seen the lawman's picture in the paper lots of times, and he was a federal agent, just like he had said. But why would Eliot Ness be standing at his door? It didn't make any more sense than Jimmy Cagney.

Then he noticed that the famous lawman had a gun drawn on him.

"Can I help you, sir?" Louis asked.

"Do you know who I am?" Ness asked him back.

Louis just shook his head. A lie didn't really count if you didn't say it out loud.

"I'm Eliot Ness," the lawman went on, slipping a badge from his pocket with his free hand and displaying it. "Does that ring any bells?"

Louis snapped his fingers. "Oh, yeah, sure. You're the guy what almost got Al Capone, except the tax men beat you to him!"

Ness gave him a scowl.

"But it was a good try," Louis added hastily, not wanting to give offense. "*Real* good."

"That *isn't* how it happened," Ness huffed. "Me and my guys did all the—Oh, never mind that, I'm not here to talk about Al Capone."

"Well, I don't know nothing about nothing, so I don't—"

Ness stepped inside and pushed the door to. He also put his gun away. "What do you know about the Bay Phantom?" he asked.

Louis tried to look stupid. "Nothing. I don't think there even is such a guy. It's just one of them stories, you know, they use it to sell papers."

Ness shook his head. "Huh-uh. Don't even try that. The Bay Phantom is real, and you know him. If he isn't and you don't, how come I saw you talking to him?"

Louis shrugged. "How should I know? You might be screwy or something, no offense. But, heck, a lotta guys look like me, and since there probably ain't no Bay Phantom, he could be anybody, so who knows? I mean, it's a funny world, ain't it?"

"Not that funny, buster. You're playing games with me. That's not smart. I'm a federal agent, Rickert."

Louis gritted his teeth and tried to smile at the same time. It probably didn't look too good. Oh, this was a hell of a mess.

"You know and I know," Ness went on, implacably, "that there *is* a Bay Phantom, and that you know him. You were down at that rescue mission with him just now."

"Rescue mission?" Louis said. "You think I look like I belong at a rescue mission? Me, with a nice disreputable suit and everything? And I guess this Bay Phantom of yours is out of work and needs a bowl of soup? You're barking up the wrong tree, Mister Ness. I been sitting right here all evening, listening to the radio. You like Jack Benny?"

"You can't bullshit me," Ness continued, "so you might as well give it up. I know he's here, or he's been here."

Louis laughed nervously.

Ness wanted to search the place, and Louis figured that might be the quickest way to get shut of him. After all, the Boss was gone, the suit wasn't up here, and there was nothing the lawman might find that would prove anything one way or the other. Anything connected with the Phantom was hidden away in a place that neither Ness nor anybody else would be able to find if they searched for a hundred years.

"Go ahead," Louis said. "You're wasting your time, but I guess that's your own business."

Ness looked around the front room. He went to both of the windows and checked those, giving Louis a couple of bad moments. Then he moved to the little bookcase that belonged to Shorty Red.

"Theodore Dreiser, Herman Melville, Jane Austen," Ness said, reading the spines of the volumes. "I know you don't read *this* stuff."

"Oh yeah?" Louis said, bristling. "Why don't I?"

"Are you kidding? You look like you'd have trouble with *Gasoline Alley*, never mind *Moby Dick*."

"There ain't no need to get vulgar. And I read *Gasoline Alley* every day."

Ness shook his head and went to the other side of the room, peering through the doors of both bedrooms.

"You got a roommate, I guess," he said.

"Yeah, I guess I do."

"Is he another cheap hood like you?"

"Naw, he ain't cheap. Listen, I know you're a big shot and everything, but you could lay off the wisecracks, I ain't never done nothing to you. You want to search the place, go on ahead and get it over with, willya?"

Louis breathed a sincere sigh of relief when Ness finally left. The lawman had obviously realized he was up against a guy who couldn't be cracked.

"I thought I'd never get rid of him," he said out loud. He went to his

"You can't bullshit me!"

room and fished under the mattress for the fifth of whiskey he kept there, so Shorty wouldn't know about it. Damn good thing that Ness character hadn't found it! He uncorked the bottle, took two deep swallows, wiped his mouth, and replaced the cork. Then he wandered around the apartment for a while, until his nerves settled down a little. He was giving some thought to making an excursion to a nearby speakeasy for a couple of beers and a plate of oysters when he remembered something important.

"Oh, hell, the Boss's suit!"

He grabbed a flashlight, dashed out the door, down the stairs, and around to the alleyway behind the building.

He spent thirty minutes, going up and down the alley from one end to the other, looking over, under, and behind every trash can, discarded crate, and pile of refuse.

No suit.

He went back upstairs to the bottle.

CHAPTER TWENTY-ONE

BUT NOW MY COURSE IS DONE

At five minutes before midnight, a guard unlocked Tom Dart's cell door and stood back to allow the warden to step in. Warden Gergan was a short, slightly rotund man. He looked more like a banker than a prison official.

"Well, son," he said. "I'm afraid it's that time."

Tom nodded and stood up from his bunk. He shook hands with the warden.

"I'm awful sorry," Gergan said. "I hate these things, you know."

"I don't like 'em too much myself," Tom said, smiling. "We could call it off if you'd like, I wouldn't complain." He felt genuinely sad for the warden and wanted to cheer him up a little if he could. He didn't think it was possible, though. Gallows humor wasn't designed to actually amuse anybody.

"The priest you asked for is here," the warden said. "Father, you can come on in."

A tall man—a little broad in the shoulders for a priest, Tom thought—stepped into the cell with a guard at his elbow. The guard was not Sander.

Tom hadn't seen that little worm since the day Maizie's remarkable letter had been delivered.

"Good evening, Thomas," said the priest. Tom studied his face. It was pale and lifeless, like a rubber mask. Only the man's eyes seemed alive.

"Father," Tom said with a nod. "Thank you for coming."

"Are any of you men Catholic?" the priest asked the group in the cell. "Are you familiar at all with the Final Sacrament?" The guards and the warden all shook their heads. The priest seemed oddly pleased by this.

"Very well, then," he said, "we shall proceed."

He placed his black bag on the cot and opened it, removing a rosary, a cup, a small decanter filled with red liquid, and a Communion wafer.

"Be at peace my son," the man said, handing the rosary to Tom. "The Lord of Hosts will keep at bay the fearful phantoms of the Adversary. Take the blood of our Savior and know that you shall not die, but be delivered unto fields of maize and seas of coral ere this day is done." He poured the liquid from the decanter into the cup and handed it to Tom. Tom gave the priest a quizzical look and took a small sip.

"Drink deep," the priest told him. "For those who consume the Blood, death is but an illusion. Be assured, my son, that you will awaken in a better place."

Then the priest winked at him. Tom drained the contents of the cup. It did not taste like wine at all. In fact, it was absolutely revolting, but he gave no sign of distaste. The priest made a few passes with his hand and touched Tom on the forehead.

Tom felt a little woozy when he stood up. A feeling of warm well-being took possession of him. It might have been the Peace of God, but it felt more like some kind of powerful anesthetic.

Two guards held onto his arms as he stepped out of the little cell for the first time in weeks—and for the last time ever.

"Hey, cop," came the voice of Lucas Horne from the adjoining cell. "Time's up now, huh?"

"Yeah, I reckon it is," Tom said.

"Well, listen, they say it's over real quick, so don't worry, okay?"

"I'll try not to." Tom moved closer to the door of Lucas's cell and peered through the little aperture. All he could see in the darkness beyond was the occupant's eyes and teeth, dimly reflecting the light from the hallway.

"Hey," said Lucas, "maybe I'll see you on the other side in a little while."

"Maybe so," Tom replied.

"Aw, who'm I kidding? They probably got a 'Colored Only' section there too."

Tom chuckled without mirth. "You take care, buddy."

"*Take care*," Lucas repeated. "You one funny cop, you know that?"

The "last mile" was only a few yards, down a cold concrete hallway to a door. The warden opened it and ushered the little party into the room. The priest kept up a steady stream of muttered prayers in what Tom figured was Latin.

The walls of the room were painted gray. The chair itself, a bulky, ugly thing, was painted a garish bright yellow. That was how the beast had come to be called "Yellow Mama." Very cute, Tom thought. Behind the chair was a small, rectangular window. Affixed to the sill, on a short metal rod, was a circular metal disk with the word "ready' etched into it. Behind the window, Tom knew, was the man who would soon be pulling the switch.

The two guards guided him to the chair and helped him sit down.

He felt strangely detached from his own body, carefree in a way he had never experienced before. Time was doing something strange, slowed nearly to a stop at the edges, rushing madly forward in the middle. He was not the slightest bit put out about being in an electric chair. The electrode being attached to his leg amused him, as did the metal band one of the guards placed around his head. Just before they dropped the black mask over his face, he winked at the priest, who nodded and smiled.

The warden was saying something about the authority of the State of Alabama and carrying out a lawful sentence. His voice came to Tom from a long way off, miles or maybe years. Tom's ear itched, but he couldn't do anything about it now. The warden told somebody to proceed.

And then...

"It seems to have worked," the Phantom said. "It really was quite simple, in spite of the extreme gravity of the situation."

They sat together in the Phantom's sedan, a little way down the road from the prison. It was an hour after Tom Dart's execution.

Mirabelle nodded. "It was risky, but at least it's moving along quickly. Not a whole lot of time to screw it up by overthinking. The less baroque the plan, the fewer opportunities to step into a pile of shit."

"Mirabelle—"

"Oh, hush. I can say *shit* as much as I want to. I've earned the right by coming up with this scheme. If it all works out, I'm gonna say *shit* every other word for a month."

"You practically do anyhow."

"Bullshit, no I don't."

There was another car, a modest T-Model Ford, parked behind them. In the back seat of that car lay Father Patrick Cavanaugh.

Mirabelle and the Phantom had lain in wait for the priest, less than a mile from the prison. When they had seen his car approaching, Mirabelle had stepped out into the road and flagged him down, giving him no choice but to stop, planting herself directly in front of the man's vehicle.

"I'm sorry, Miss," he had said, when she came around to the driver's side window, "but I have an appointment that *must* be kept."

"So have I," Mirabelle had replied, raising a small spray gun and hitting the priest in the face with a blast of anesthetic gas.

"I made sure Tom requested this particular priest," Mirabelle had said, as she and the Phantom removed him from the T-Model. "He has kind of a reputation." She had raised a hand to her mouth, thumb extended, to pantomime drinking from a bottle. "He won't remember a thing. He'll wake up in his own bed and he won't dare tell anybody that he blacked out."

They had placed the unconscious man of the cloth in the back seat of the sedan. The Phantom, made up by Mirabelle to pass for the priest, had then driven the T-Model to the prison.

When he had returned, after the execution, he and Mirabelle had returned the slumbering Father to his own car.

"I hated doing this to an innocent man of the cloth," the Phantom said as they sat waiting.

"Nobody is innocent," Mirabelle remarked. "Anything bad that happens to anybody is merely justice getting lucky."

"I know you don't believe that. Why do you say such things?"

"You don't know what I believe. Now quit talking and be still, so I can get this damn makeup off you."

"I'm not too happy about having profaned a sacred ceremony," the Phantom said as Mirabelle worked, "but I had to deliver some reassurance to poor Tom, so I altered the formula for the Final Sacrament. You weren't able to give him too many details in that coded letter you had Maizie write. I did my best to let him know it was me, and that the situation was under control."

"I'm sure you were just fine, and I doubt God will hold your profanation against you."

"You don't believe in God."

"Well, if there was one, you'd have no cause for concern. I hope you're not thinking about telling all this to that Archbishop of yours."

"I don't know. I haven't had much time to think about such things, what with all that's been going on."

"I would advise you to stay away from him in the future. It may be okay, you talking to him once, but I'd hate to see you make a habit of it."

The Phantom did not reply.

They waited until a hearse passed them, headed back toward Mobile.

"There he goes," Mirabelle said, slipping out of the sedan. "We better get moving."

Mirabelle drove the priest's car back to Mobile, with the Phantom following in his own automobile. She parked outside the man's residence and the Phantom helped her carry him up to his room and tuck him into bed.

Their next stop was the Baker Funeral Home on South Broad Street, close to the Magnolia Cemetery. The hearse had been and gone, and the lone employee who had received the body had locked up and gone home half an hour before they arrived.

After making sure the place was unoccupied by anyone living, the Phantom gained entry to the building and left the rear door propped open, then returned to the car to help Mirabelle extract a large object wrapped in a sheet from the from the trunk. They carried the object into the building.

"This is the worst part of your plan," the Phantom grumbled as they maneuvered the thing in through a rear door. "I wish you could have devised something that didn't necessitate grave robbing."

"Swiping a body from the city morgue is hardly robbing a grave," she said dismissively. "We're lucky Chester was able to get me an impression of the key. If they didn't have anything to bury, there would be way too many questions. What did you want me to do, grow one in a Petri dish?"

"Of course not."

"And they'll never miss it because I stole the paperwork as well. It'll be put down as a clerical error. Be careful with it. It took me six hours to make that thing look enough like Tom Dart to pass mortuary muster. Now quit fussing and help me get Tom out of that casket."

They unscrewed the lid of the inexpensive wooden casket. The Phantom produced a flashlight and shined the beam on Tom's face.

"He looks a bit pasty," he observed.

"Try getting electrocuted and see how you look," Mirabelle replied. "He looks just like he's supposed to."

She performed a quick examination, and said, "His vital signs are in suspension, but he'll come around quickly when I give him the other serum, and a mild electrical shock to restart his heart. He's alive, Joe, he's just hibernating."

They lifted Tom out of the box and placed him gingerly on an unoccupied metal table.

The Phantom removed the sheet from the substitute body and held it in his arms, studying it in the dim light. "You did a good job on this poor fellow," he allowed. "If I didn't know Tom very well, it might fool me."

"Well, thank you."

"You say he was found dead of a drug overdose in an abandoned house?"

"According to the paperwork, yeah."

The Phantom shook his head sadly. "Well, perhaps his spirit can take solace in the fact that his body is being used to help right a terrible injustice."

"I'm sure it will. Now put him in this thing and let's get the lid back on."

Once the substitute corpse was securely nestled into the cheap casket, Mirabelle and the Phantom carried Tom out to the car and laid him across the back seat.

"That was the hard part," Mirabelle said as she put the car into gear.

"If you say so," said the Phantom.

"I do," Mirabelle said, nodding her head sharply.

CHAPTER TWENTY-TWO

AND NOW IS MY REWARD

"Coral and Maizie are asleep," Winona told them when they arrived back at Tull House.

"Good," said Mirabelle. "We're going to take Tom down to the laboratory, and the next half hour will tell the tale."

The Phantom carried his friend from the car, into the house, and down into Mirabelle's laboratory in the warren of secret rooms underneath Tull House.

"Just put him there on that table," Mirabelle said. "This won't take long."

Mirabelle had studied a number of formulae she had obtained from Doctor Piranha while he had been out of prison. Piranha had come up with a number of ways to enhance various aspects of human endurance and performance. Piranha's experiments had been responsible for the Phantom's stamina and rapid healing, and also for the Werewolf's superhuman strength and savagery.

By isolating a few factors she uncovered in Piranha's notes, she had developed a serum that would, for a very limited time, allow a person to survive an electrocution. She had told Perrone that she had experimented on mice, which was true. But what she had omitted to tell him was that she had also experimented on herself. Of course, she had not subjected herself to the amount of current Tom would receive, but she had done enough to make sure that her science was sound. Perrone would have questioned her sanity, and she didn't need any help doing that.

Now it was time for her to prove that her madness had method.

First, she used a very long hypodermic needle to inject something directly into Tom's heart. Then she attached electrodes to his head and chest. Moving to a control panel against the wall, she threw a few switches and a low hum filled the room.

"Awaken," Mirabelle intoned in a sepulchral voice. "Awaken and arise. Come forth, Tom Dart!"

"Mirabelle, there's no need to blaspheme."

"Hush, I'm having fun. Look, he's moving! His hand twitched! He's alive, *alive*!" She jumped up and down and clapped her hands together wildly.

The Phantom tsk-tsked and shook his head, but he felt a surge of excitement as he watched Tom's arms twitch. His heart leapt when the "dead man's" eyelids fluttered then opened wide.

"Ghaaaa!" Tom yelled, sitting abruptly upright. He looked wildly around the laboratory, an expression of near-panic on his pale face.

"It's all right, Tom," the Phantom said. "It's me. I'm here with you. You're safe."

Tom Dart stared at the masked man. He reached out a hand, slowly, tentatively, then drew it back.

"I need to check his vital signs," Mirabelle said. "And probably administer a mild sedative."

Tom Dart appeared confused and possibly on the edge of total panic, but remained docile enough as Mirabelle checked his temperature, heart rate, and blood pressure, then gave him a shot of something. Gradually, Tom grew calmer and more lucid. He looked at the Phantom and nodded.

"Christ, it is you," he said. "I guess it worked, huh? I'm not in prison any more and I'm not dead."

"That's right," the masked man confirmed.

"Well—Thanks for getting me out."

"You're more than welcome. Actually, the thanks should go to my friend Mirabelle, here. She engineered the whole thing. I don't believe you've met. Mirabelle, Tom Dart; Tom Dart, Mirabelle. I omit her surname because we tend to be a bit secretive down here, you understand."

Tom laughed. It sounded strained and awkward, a thing he had almost forgotten how to do.

"Glad to meet you, Miss," he said, shaking Mirabelle's hand. "So you raise people from the dead, eh?"

Mirabelle was relieved. In fact, she and Tom Dart *had* met, during the Cannibal Guild affair—one of those things Joe Perrone did not need to know about. Fortunately, Tom had either forgotten about it in the excitement of his "resurrection," or he sensed that some things were better left unmentioned.

"No," she said. "I just help them survive electrocutions, that's all. But, as far as the State of Alabama is concerned, you are dead, and you'll have to stay that way, at least until—"

"Oh my God!" Tom blurted, memory hitting him like an anvil dropped from three stories up, "Maizie and Coral! I have to—"

"It's okay, Tom,' the Phantom assured him. "Your wife and daughter are fine. They're here with us. You can see them soon."

Mirabelle removed the electrodes, ran a few tests on Tom, and made him drink a vitamin concoction that nearly turned his stomach.

His muscles ached as though from a long day of unaccustomed hard labor, and his throat burned a little when he breathed. But he could breathe, he was alive, and there was nary an iron bar in sight. The dank hell of the prison was no longer wrapped around him, he was free of the sounds and the smells and the air as thick as a mildewed wool blanket, and it felt wonderful.

The Phantom brought him some clothes to wear, a gray flannel shirt and a pair of dungarees.

There would certainly be complications in the days to come, but he didn't have the desire or the energy to fret over those right now. This freedom, after all the horrible months, was too sweet not to savor to the fullest.

And it soon got sweeter, when the Phantom escorted Maizie and Coral into the lab.

Mirabelle excused herself and went to her own small laboratory, while the Phantom simply disappeared, leaving the little family to enjoy their reunion in private.

The following day, Perrone, in his Bay Phantom outfit, paid a "visit" to Tull House, and spoke with Tom Dart's wife and daughter.

"Maizie, you and Coral will have to attend Tom's funeral, I think," the Phantom said. They had left Tom down in the laboratory to enjoy a few hours of sedated sleep, and were sitting in the living room up in Tull House. "The whole situation is suspicious enough; we need to avoid whatever irregularities we can. I hope it won't be too upsetting."

"Are you kidding? I'll enjoy it, knowing Tom's back here, safe. It might be a little confusing for Coral, though." She turned to the little girl. "Honey, you understand that Daddy is alive and okay, don't you? You saw him. And the funeral we go to will be just pretend, right?"

Coral nodded. "Yeah, Mommy, I get it. Daddy got broke out of that goddamn jail 'cause he was in there on a bum rap, and we gotta make everybody think he's dead until the Phantom can catch up with the assholes that framed him."

"Coral! Where did you pick up such language?"

"Miss Mirabelle."

The Phantom looked at Mirabelle. The mask and goggles did nothing to hide the scowl he was aiming her way.

"She must have overheard me talking to Winona," she said sheepishly. "I'm sorry."

Maizie laughed. She stood up, went over to Mirabelle, and put her arms around her. "Oh, Mirabelle," she said, "you will never, ever have to apologize to me for anything."

After Maizie sat back down, Mirabelle gestured to the Phantom to follow her into the hallway.

"I need to talk to you," she whispered.

"Do you have some colorful new terms you'd like to teach me?"

"Very cute. No, I finished analyzing that dust you brought from the rescue mission. You'll never guess what it is."

"Then tell me."

"Uranium."

"Really?"

She nodded. "That ties in with what Chester said about what they found at the scenes of those murders. So there's definitely a connection between the killings and that rescue mission. What it might be, I cannot imagine."

"Nor can I."

CHAPTER TWENTY-THREE

THE SUIT 2

Rickey Harvard was a very happy young man. He looked around his fine new room, at the nice console radio and the pretty red curtains and the comfortable, four-poster bed. He had sure come a long way since that last night he'd been at St. Dymphna's.

After the fight at the rescue mission, Rickey had wandered about for a little while, just barely getting clear of the place before the cops showed up. He had spotted a couple of guys walking together, and a third man a good distance behind them, apparently following them. Rickey trailed along, for want of any other direction to go in. They walked through Bienville Square and across Conception Street, taking a right up Dauphin Street. Rickey, wanting to avoid the street lights, ducked around into the alley that ran behind Dauphin.

He had remained still for a few minutes in the shadows, until he was certain he was safe. Then he started moving toward the far end of the alley.

It was while he was passing below a lighted window that something had hit him square on the head. At first he had thought he'd been jumped on by some mugger, and had whirled around and swung his fists.

Nobody hit him back and he soon realized he was just fighting with a bundle of cloth.

It was a fine suit, and probably very expensive. And with a cape, no less! He probably wouldn't get much use out of that, but it would be nice to have one, like for Halloween or something.

And a nice hat too. It was a little bunged-up, but that would be easy to fix.

Why had someone just thrown all of it away? Well, whatever the case, it was a bit of rare good fortune for Rickey.

He had bundled it up, tucked it under his arm, and continued on his way to his current residence, an abandoned house on Tarrant Street where he had been squatting for the past few weeks

The neighborhood was neither bad nor good, really. In fact, it wasn't really a neighborhood at all, since there were no neighbors. All the houses on that part of the street were empty, some of them serving as temporary refuge for derelicts.

Rickey had lit a candle and, in the dim illumination, examined his find

The cape was strong, but very thin, made out of some kind of fabric Rickey had never seen before, and it fit into a little pouch inside the back part of the jacket.

The suit wasn't a bad fit. The trousers had been a little bit long, but they could easily be hemmed up by a tailor. The jacket had fit pretty much perfectly. Rickey had rather long arms. His father always said that came from his mother's side of the family, because they were just a bunch of goddamn baboons.

But that wasn't all. There were some hidden pockets as well, in the front of the jacket, and it was in these that he made his most interesting discoveries.

The first was a gun. And not just any old gun, but a shiny .45 automatic, fully loaded. Rickey handled it like it was a combination of a poisonous snake and a golden idol, awed by the power and majesty of the thing.

The second was the mask with attached goggles. They had looked familiar to him, but his mind hadn't been working too well, and he had set them aside.

The third find hadn't been in the jacket. Examining the trousers, Rickey had discovered a huge roll of bills pinned into the hip pocket. Most were twenties, but there were a few fifties and even a couple of hundreds. He had nearly passed out with emotion. It was more money than he had ever had in his whole life put together, and here it was, all in one place, and it was his.

The money had changed everything. After buying a nice pair of shoes, a shirt, and a tie, and getting his trousers hemmed up, Rickey had moved out of the abandoned house and into the Battle House Hotel downtown. Something had just put the idea into his head, and it had been a good one. It was a swell place. Eight stories tall! Rickey got a room on the sixth floor, with a big window looking down on North Royal Street. The lobby of the building had a domed skylight and fancy paintings all over the ceiling and walls, pictures of various kings or people from the Bible or something. Very elegant, at any rate, and Rickey's room had its own toilet and bathtub, as well as a radio.

The hotel had been there since 1908. There had been another Battle House before that, on the same spot, and that one had been built in 1852, but had burned down in 1905. There was a little plaque in the lobby telling the whole story, and Rickey read it over several times, proud to be making his home in such an interesting place. Rickey had always figured the hotel had been named after some Civil War battle, or maybe all of them, but according to the plaque it was named after the guys who had built the first one, James Battle and his half-nephews John and Samuel. Rickey wasn't sure what a half-nephew might be, and he pictured a couple of poor crippled fellows.

After he had settled into the hotel and his fine new life, he turned his thoughts to the mask and goggles.

Rickey never paid much attention to the news, so he was only vaguely aware of the Bay Phantom, and had never known until now what the crime fighter looked like. It was hard not to, nowadays, with the masked man's picture in the papers every day. Rickey had never been much of a reader, but since his stroke of good fortune, he had been buying the paper every day, just like all the other guests did, and it was impossible not to learn a little bit about what was going on.

Some people were saying the Bay Phantom was a vicious killer. The police were after him, as a matter of fact. But most people still believed he was a hero. As a few folks in the newspapers and on the radio had pointed out, it wouldn't be the first time the Phantom had been accused of something he hadn't done.

It was the pictures, though, that had the biggest impact on Rickey. The Bay Phantom looked exactly like the "ghost" he had seen on two different occasions, in two different cemeteries, over the past year.

This put things in a whole new light. What if it *hadn't* been a ghost he had seen in those two cemeteries? It seemed likely now that what he had actually seen was the Bay Phantom.

And now, through some kind of miracle, he had come into possession of the Bay Phantom's suit and mask. For a short time, he wondered if maybe the Bay Phantom had been killed and God had picked him out to be the new Bay Phantom.

That didn't seem too likely, though. There was probably some other explanation for it, and he might find it out some day.

Well, either way, he had a fine suit and plenty of cash. He could go out and hunt a job pretty soon, but for now, he figured he had a right to enjoy himself for a while.

CHAPTER TWENTY-FOUR

YOU CAN'T GO HOME AGAIN

The Embalmer had been having odd dreams. One of the central figures was a hollow woman. She seemed familiar, he was certain he knew her from somewhere, but he could not place her. She was very important, though. He was connected to her in some way. In one of the dreams, he met her in a large stone building, and together they fought an octopus. In another, they sat in a dark room and played a game of chess, using tiny human corpses as pieces. The corpses didn't seem quite dead, though; they rolled their little eyes and their hands and feet twitched as they were moved around on the board. Not only that, but they spoke too:

"Who is like unto the beast? Who is able to make war with him?"

The Embalmer couldn't decipher the odd dreams, but he knew they must mean something. He needed to move forward with his plans. That was what the dreams must be telling him.

He discussed the matter with Paul over the dinner table.

"I think I should go see him,' said the Embalmer. "Just to kind of get his reaction to my plans."

"The Bay Phantom you mean?" Paul asked. "You think that's a good idea? I mean, from what you've told me—"

"Oh, he'll balk at first, sure. But he'll get used to it. I have to think he'll welcome an ally in his crusade. Especially now, with all these ghastly murders going on. If nothing else, I need to check in with him so he won't blame *me* for them."

"Because you used to kill people, like you told me."

"Yes. But, to be fair, the people I killed were, for the most part, other criminals. Not innocent citizens by any stretch of the imagination. In any event, I must talk with my friend, the Phantom. It's been too long since we had one of our chats. But before I do anything else, there are a few things I need to retrieve. I require some inspiration for my new course in life, and I hope I may find it among them. Items that have sentimental value, mostly."

"Retrieve from where?"

"A little hideaway I used to maintain in the Cathedral Basilica of the Immaculate Conception."

The Cathedral Basilica of the Immaculate Conception. A landmark in downtown Mobile. He had experienced a strong compulsion to come here at this particular time. It seemed that he had heard voices telling him to do so, but that had not really been a deciding factor, since he constantly heard voices telling him to do this or that. But the feeling had been so powerful today that he had not dared disobey it.

The Embalmer found the secret entrance he had used once upon a time. No one had found it in all the months since he'd last used it. His old laboratory, down by the crypts, was still there, untouched. Someone had uncovered one of his other nooks—the one he had designed to be found if his cover was ever blown—but they never located this one. That was nice. Dust, being dust, had gathered over everything, of course.

He must have spent time in this cathedral when he was a child. He couldn't remember it. He had memories of a Catholic education, but those memories were elusive. Some were quite vivid, others were nebulous. He remembered the nuns. Fearsome creatures they had been, with their talk of suffering and damnation, and the heavy rulers they swung with gleeful abandon at the tender knuckles of their innocent students.

It looked as though some work had been done on the building recently, and he hoped his little secrets had not been cracked open.

Being back here awakened a sense of nostalgia that he was surprised to find he possessed. He missed the old place. He had spent many happy, solitary hours here, making plans, designing and building new equipment, conducting interesting chemical experiments.

Not that there was much left now. Just a few useless pieces of equipment and some old magazines. He pocketed a few trinkets that were part of his confused personal history, none of them particularly worth the trouble it had taken to reach them, unfortunately. But there was one item that he wanted to be sure he took with him. He found it where he had left it, hidden in the back of a desk drawer.

It was a heavy wooden ruler, darkened with age and with the blood of innocents. How many tiny knuckles had been shattered by this abominable implement? The thing had surely never done an honest day's measuring.

This was the very ruler that a certain Sister Mary Humilitas had used on his knuckles when he had been a schoolboy.

He was sure that had happened. The memory was seared into his brain, as fresh now as it had been all those years ago. He had learned something valuable from the experience, though he wasn't certain what that was. But it had made such an impression on him that he had stolen the ruler from her desk and held onto it for all these years. He tucked the precious relic away inside his shirt.

He wondered if his other secret passages were still intact. He used to spend hours prowling around the old building, inside the walls and ceilings. It made him feel like an insect. He had always rather admired insects, and had experienced sharp pangs of envy toward Gregor Samsa when he read Kafka's "The Metamorphosis."

To his delight, he found most of the old passageways just as he remembered them, perhaps a bit more dusty from disuse.

He prowled around for the better part of an hour, working his way up and back, until he found himself in the section of the building that was given over to various offices.

This part of the building must have been renovated recently. Here, he left his old secret passages behind and wormed his way into some duct work, which seemed to be relatively new. It wasn't exactly roomy, but it presented no insurmountable obstacles.

He crept around for a while, seeing nothing of interest, until he came to one of the offices near the western wall on the uppermost floor.

"Let's talk about this, Kraken."

...old passageways as he remembered...

A voice he had heard before, long ago. Suddenly, something in his head cracked open and a small flood of memories.

"That's old Father Craig," he whispered to himself as he slithered closer to the vent.

The slats were situated in such a way that he couldn't see anything but a tiny sliver of the room, just enough to tell that the old man was standing in front of an open closet door.

He thought hard about old Father Craig. Yes, he did remember the man. Back when the Embalmer had been a child, during the time of Sister Mary Humilitas and her ruler, Father Craig had been his parish priest. That was when he had been friends with that terrible boy whose name he still couldn't recall, the one who had gotten him interested in chemical experiments. Old Father Craig was an Archbishop now, wasn't he?

"The Perrone problem is getting worse, it's true," said old Father or Archbishop Craig. "But I still think we can turn it to our advantage."

Perrone. The Embalmer turned the name over and over in his mind. It had some significance, didn't it? He was sure that it did.

"He needs to be eliminated," said another voice. This one was raspy and dry, nothing like Craig's voice, which the Embalmer would describe as dulcet, or possibly mellifluous. Was he talking to someone in the closet?

"I... I would hesitate to do that," Father Craig replied. "He's a good boy, I've known him for such a long time, and he does mean well."

"He could destroy everything we've been working for," croaked the other. "The Bay Phantom is dangerous, and you know it."

Did he say the Bay Phantom? What's going on here? Why is old Father Craig discussing my dear friend with a malevolent frog?

"I suppose so," Craig said. "Perhaps we could throw a scare into him."

"I don't think so. You think a man like that could be frightened away? He and his friends destroyed the International Patriots Guild, did they not? And the new Klan before that?"

Craig sighed. "Yes, that's true. But, as it turned out, the Guild *needed* to be destroyed, didn't it? They didn't tell us what their real objective was when we agreed to help them. Kebler and Till were madmen. The Phantom and his associates did us a service."

"Pure chance. Perrone must be destroyed. You know I'm right, Craig. This is bigger than just you an me. The whole Anti-Diocese of Mobile is in peril, even as we move into the final phases of our grand plan. You know this, Craig."

Another sigh from Craig, this one deeper and filled with regret.

"Of course you know best, Kraken."

"Tomorrow night. At his house. I'll give the orders, since you seem to lack the will. I will deal with Perrone."

"But Kraken—Consider this: If we could convince him of the rightness of our cause, he could be a very powerful ally. He is not as self-righteous as he may seem. I know he has doubts about himself and what he does. We should at least give him an opportunity."

"I think you're being foolish, Craig, but... I suppose you'll give me no peace unless I indulge you."

"You'll see, Kraken. Joe Perrone will listen to reason."

Joe Perrone! The Embalmer knew who that was. Of course. That was the name of the man who owned that peculiar house out on the Bay, the one where the Phantom evidently spent a great deal of time. The Embalmer had once made his way there through one of the Phantom's tunnels, the one that came out at the Church Street Grave Yard. It had not occurred to the Embalmer before, as far as he could recall, but Perrone and the Phantom were probably one and the same.

Oh, this is providential indeed. Anybody who doesn't believe in Providence ought to be jammed here into this ductwork with me.

"I'll give him a chance," came the harsh croak of Kraken. "But I won't dilly around forever. Tomorrow night. I'll go see him myself, at his house, and show him what he's dealing with. Tomorrow night at eight. You will make the arrangements. Now leave me alone. I must think."

"As you say Kraken," Craig said. He closed the closet door.

The Embalmer backtracked down through the ductwork and into his old network of secret passages. From there, he made his way back to his old headquarters, then out of the building.

As he sat on a bench in the small courtyard out back, his mind was racing.

They're going to strike tomorrow night, at that house where the Phantom and/or Perrone lives. I can find the place again, I know I can. Well, this is a good opportunity, isn't it? To be a crime fighter I mean, because this Kraken character is certainly a criminal.

I can't fight crime as the Black Embalmer, though. That bridge has been burned. I need something new. Something with some real pizzazz. Being a bit of a criminal myself, I ought to be able to come up with something that will strike a chord.

And what do I know about criminals? Well, apart from myself, they tend to be on the cowardly side, not to mention prone to superstition. Yes, a superstitious and cowardly lot they are, on the whole. They are rowdy and given to hooliganism, utterly lacking in self-discipline. I must craft a new persona, one that will strike terror into their hearts. I must be something black and terrible, something that will—

At that moment, a group of four nuns emerged from the rear of the cathedral and descended the steps, chattering together, probably about the most effective methods for destroying young people's knuckles with their horrible wooden rulers. He watched them for a few moments, until a sudden light dawned on his face.

That's it!

He looked at the ruler in his hand, hefted it, and smiled.

CHAPTER TWENTY-FIVE

ATTACK ON TULL HOUSE

"There's a bunch of weird bums outside," Coral Dart said.

"What's that, honey?" Maizie asked.

"Weird bums," the little girl repeated. "I think they're drunk. Come look at them."

Joe Perrone, Mirabelle Darcy, and the Dart family had been sitting around the dining table off the kitchen in Tull House, discussing recent developments. Tom was feeling much better, and had finally been brought upstairs. Perrone had explained to him that his good friend, The Bay Phantom, maintained his headquarters underneath Tull House, which was really stretching it, as far as Mirabelle was concerned, but if Tom was as dubious as any sane person would have been, he gave no sign. Coral had wandered off into the front room, and come back a few minutes later with her information.

The adults rose from the table and followed her back to the front room. Mirabelle and Perrone went to the front window, pulled back the curtains, and peered out.

There were eight of them out on the lawn. They moved stiffly, shuffling through the grass, heading toward the front door, unhurried but implacable. Each of them held a long-bladed knife.

"What the hell is this?" Mirabelle said.

"I think you'd better hit the switch, Mirabelle," Perrone said.

Mirabelle went to an ornate old clock on the wall and pushed it to the left, revealing a small, square recess into which had been set a switch. Mirabelle pulled it down. A low hum sounded throughout the house as the lights dimmed and slatted steel shutters slammed into place over all the doors and windows, rattling and clashing dramatically as every possible entrance was mechanically secured.

Perrone stepped into the hallway and ducked inside a small cupboard. When he emerged a moment later, he was attired in the suit, cloak, and mask of the Bay Phantom.

"Well," said Tom Dart.

"Uh-huh," said Maizie Dart.

"Wowee!" exclaimed Coral Dart, clapping her hands together.

"You certainly surmised this before now, Tom, Maizie," the Phantom said. "And now it is confirmed. Joe Perrone is the Bay Phantom. I know I can trust you with the information."

"What about me?" Coral asked.

"Oh, of course I can trust you, Coral," the Phantom said, smiling behind his mask. "It was so obvious, it just went without saying. Now, I think you had best let your mother take you to one of our secure rooms while we tend to the, ah, weird bums."

"Aw, I wanna help."

"You can help from behind the scenes," the masked man said. "We need to have forces in reserve, and that will be you. I need you to make sure that room remains in perfect order, and I know I can count on you."

"All right, sir. I'll do my best."

"Good. Mirabelle, show Maizie and Coral to the safe room. Tom, you stay with me and let's see if we can't form a quick plan of action."

"You be careful," Maizie said. "I just got you back."

Just as Mirabelle returned to the front room, carrying an armload of rifles she had taken from a reinforced closet in the hallway, Winona Dirge came down the stairs.

"What's going on, Mirabelle? I was taking a bath and all of a sudden the lights started blinking and something slid down over the window!" She took note of the Phantom and said, "Oh, hi."

The Phantom turned around from where he'd been peering out between the steel slats that covered the front window, nodded politely, and said, "Good evening, Miss."

"Winona Dirge, Bay Phantom; Bay Phantom, Winona Dirge," Mirabelle said quickly, hoping the identity question wouldn't come up again right away. "We've got a kind of situation here, and he, ah, *very* fortunately showed up to, ah, help."

"Oh, sure," Winona said. "That's a nice outfit, Mister Perrone. So, what's the deal?" She cracked her knuckles. "I can help too—*very* fortunately."

Mirabelle threw up her hands. "Come tomorrow, there won't be anyone left who *doesn't* know!"

"It's all right, Mirabelle," said the Phantom. "I'm sure she's trustworthy."

Mirabelle handed guns to everyone in the room, keeping one for herself and propping the two extras against a sofa.

"If it was just those poor derelicts, I wouldn't be so concerned," the Phantom said. "But there's someone else back there on the road. Those men are a distraction."

Indeed, Mirabelle saw that there were two vehicles out on the road—a van and a pickup truck. Someone in a long robe was standing up in the rear of the latter, arms raised. The robed figure was flanked by two men with shotguns.

Two men climbed out of the van and strode toward the house, walking purposefully between the shamblers.

It was the tall man and the short man, Jack Foregone and Mark Mills—the Scarecrow and the Mouse. Both of them wore dark protective goggles, they were lugging a piece of heavy equipment between them, a large, boxy thing with what appeared to be a pair of oxygen tanks attached to it. They set it down on the porch, and Forgone detached a nozzle which was connected to a short hose.

"Holy crap," Mirabelle said. "That's an oxy acetylene torch."

The Mouse reached into his jacket pocket and produced a friction lighter. The Scarecrow made some adjustments to the mechanism attached to the tanks, then took the lighter and ignited the torch, and applied the white-hot flame to the metal slats over the front door.

"They came prepared," the Phantom observed.

"Sort of," Mirabelle said. "What's to stop us from shooting them through the slats?"

"Apart from common decency, you mean?"

"I doubt that enters into any of their calculations. Maybe they're just stupid."

"I rather doubt that. Bulletproof undergarments, maybe? Or perhaps they... Well, what I think I'll do is—"

Mirabelle poked his arm. "Wait. Look there."

A small roadster had pulled up out on the road, behind the truck from which the "zombies" were seemingly being directed. A strange figure hopped out of the car and walked toward the other vehicle.

"Is that a *nun*?" Mirabelle asked.

The newcomer was clad in what certainly appeared to be a nun's habit, a voluminous black garment covered with intricate designs in gold stitching, with a swath of white lace across the bosom. The face was quite remarkable. It was dead white and wore a fixed expression that conveyed nothing. And topping off the ensemble was a Thompson submachine gun carried in the crook of one arm.

"I do believe it is," the Phantom said. He pressed his masked face closer to the window, peering through the steel slats. "You know, there's something awfully familiar about—Oh my goodness, it can't be. But I'm sure it is."

"What?" Mirabelle said, shaking his shoulder. "What is it?"

"That posture, the way the figure moves. I know who that is, Mirabelle. And you do too. Just take a good look."

She pressed her head up close to his. "Hmm. That really looks like—" She shook her head. "Oh, shit, no."

"I'm afraid so."

"He sure loves those porcelain masks, doesn't he? At least this one's an improvement. Sort of."

The "nun" had stopped near the pickup truck and raised the machine gun. The men standing in the bed had not yet noticed the strange interloper.

"Oh, dear," said the Phantom. "I'd better get out there. I'll use the emergency tunnel."

"Hang on a second. I think it's too late to stop whatever he's about to do, and I don't want you getting caught in the middle of it."

The robed figure on the back of the truck noticed the Nun at that moment, saw what the Nun was holding, and dropped face-first into the truck bed just as the bullets began to fly. Lead slugs spanged off the rear of the pickup, sending sparks. The other two men pitched over to join their leader in the truck bed. It was unclear to the observers in the house whether or not the men had been struck by bullets.

"I mean," Mirabelle went on, "he might just solve this problem for us."

"You know better than that," said the Phantom. "He can be trusted within certain parameters. This does not lie within those. I hope he's by himself."

"What do you mean by that?" Mirabelle asked, but the Phantom was already gone.

Having quelled the men in the truck, the Nun turned his attention to the shambling figures in the front yard of Tull House. They didn't seem to have enough presence of mind to be held responsible for their actions, but that didn't mean they didn't constitute a serious threat.

He felt that the best course would be to mow them all down, but he didn't think the Phantom would approve. He kept the machine gun trained on the truck so nobody there got any funny ideas, and reached into his habit for a gas grenade. He tossed it into the middle of the shambling men. It detonated and released a thick cloud of knockout gas. The Nun held his breath and waited for it to take effect.

And waited.

And waited.

"Well, damn," he said, as he watched the men advance toward the house. "Bad batch I guess."

But that could not be. The slight breeze had caused the gas to drift away from the house, over the two vehicles, and he saw the drivers slumped in their seats, unconscious.

Well, there was no point worrying about it now. Anyhow, it seemed more important to take care of those characters trying to cut open the front door. The gas hadn't reached them, and the Nun had no more of it. He wasn't sure how the Phantom would feel about lethal violence right on what was probably his own front porch, so he decided to get closer before committing to a course of action.

He moved toward the house, shoving and kicking the strange, shambling men out of his path.

The two fellows on the porch were intent on their work. They seemed not to have noticed the gunfire earlier, though he didn't see how that was possible. The Nun crept up to the porch and silently ascended the steps. He reached into his habit and drew out the ruler. When he was directly behind the men, who had cut through one end of one of the metal bars, and were adjusting position to cut it loose, he reached out with the ruler and rapped the tall one hard on the shoulder.

"What the hell is this?" he demanded. "Do you have permission to do that?" He stepped back, out of arm's reach of the two miscreants, hefting the ruler in one hand, cradling the machine gun in the other arm.

The Scarecrow turned around and gawked for a moment. He let the torch go out, pulled down his goggles, and removed a pair of earplugs. The little guy did likewise.

"Ah, earplugs!" the Nun exclaimed. "That's one mystery cleared up. I guess you were going to use dynamite or something if that torch didn't work. Or maybe you just have very sensitive ears. Do torches make too much noise for you?"

The two men remained frozen while the Nun spoke, stunned by the weird apparition. Jack Foregone recovered first, reaching into his jacket for his gun.

Mindful of the fact that he was probably on the Bay Phantom's property, the Nun refrained from blasting the tall man into gooey fragments with the machine gun. Instead, he balanced the ruler in his hand and flung it like a boomerang. One of the sharp edges entered Foregone's right eye. The man dropped his gun, and the Nun dashed forward and scooped it up, tossing it away into one of the bushes that bordered the porch as the smaller man went for his own piece. With his free hand, he jerked the ruler out of Forgone's eye socket. The resulting jet of blood splattered the little fellow in the face, disorienting him enough for the Nun to relieve him of his revolver. A swift kick to the temple sent the Mouse into dreamland.

The Scarecrow was down on his hands and knees, crawling aimlessly and wailing about his poor eye.

"No sense crying over spilled milk, Cyclops," the Nun said, rapping the Scarecrow over the head several times with the ruler. It wasn't heavy enough to knock the man out, but the Nun's booted right foot was, and he used it for that purpose.

"You'll think twice next time before you use a blowtorch to play ding-dong ditch," he said.

The Phantom emerged from his secret tunnel, climbing out of a hollow, artificial tree on the other side of the road from Tull House. Behind him, a narrow strip of sand led down to the dark, still water of the Mobile Bay.

He crossed the road and headed for the front door of Tull House, ignoring the vehicles and the shambling men, who seemed to have lost what little sense of purpose they might have had. He approached the tableau on the porch. The Nun was examining the two unconscious men. The Phantom cleared his throat.

"Hello," he said.

"Hi there," said the Nun, turning around and waving. "Nice to see you. I suppose you know who I am."

"I figured it out, yes," said the Phantom. "That's an interesting ensemble you've got there."

Seen up close, the mask was startlingly eerie. Dead white, with wide, staring eyes. The carved expression might have been one of amusement, terror, or colossal indifference.

"Oh, thank you!" the Nun said humbly. "I call myself the Nun now. There's rather a long story behind it."

"I imagine there would have to be. Well, you seem to have taken care of these two. Very impressive. I haven't been able to do much with them. I did shoot the little one, but he got away again."

"I've always said you take too gentle an approach, even with bullet holes. One through the head would have kept him out of mischief for good."

"Hm. Well, thank you for your help. How did you happen to show up here at just the right time?"

"There's a story behind that too. But it isn't very interesting. What is interesting is what I heard last night. I was—"

"Ahoy there!" came a harsh voice from the road. The Phantom and the Nun turned.

The strange robed figure stood once more in the bed of the pickup truck, waving his arms.

Flanking this specter were the two men with shotguns, both of them aimed directly at the Phantom and the Nun.

"The gas wore off, I guess," said the Nun.

"Come here a moment," said the robed man. "And kindly drop your weapons. I wish to speak with you. If you behave yourselves, you will not be harmed."

"What should we do?" the Nun whispered.

"As he says—for now,' the Phantom responded. The Nun dropped the machine gun, and the two costumed men approached the truck.

"Hello, Mister Bay Phantom," said the robed man. "We meet at last."

"I wasn't aware that we were anticipating a meeting," the Phantom said. "Who might you be?

"I am Archbishop Kraken," said the man.

He was absolutely ghoulish-looking. His visage was as drawn and brittle-looking as the face of a mummy, the skin was a dusty purple color, and the eyes were completely yellow—no irises or pupils. In addition to the robe, he wore a mitre on his head. On the front of it was a skull and crossbones.

"How extraordinary," said the Phantom. "What, precisely, are you the Archbishop of?"

"I know who you are," said Kraken, ignoring the question. "I am in favor of your elimination, but I have been forced to argue against another faction who wishes to preserve your life."

"I see," said the Phantom. "I suppose I'm fortunate to have an advocate, then."

"I would advise you not to be flippant. This is serious, *Joseph.* Yes, I know who you are, as I said. I know all about you. We are going to make you an offer. We will offer you great power, power beyond anything you could dream of. You can learn much from us. We can change everything for you; lift you out of the foolish games you play. The offer will not last for very long, and if you refuse or allow it to expire, you and all of your friends will be destroyed. That is the outcome I expect, but I have agreed to give you your chance. We control this town, Joseph, and we will soon control much more. We can dispose of you even more easily than we did the uncooperative Tom Dart. We needed to make an example of him. *You* can simply disappear.

"I will leave you now. I know who you are and where you are, you have seen that. You cannot find me. If you did, it would be by pure, blind chance—a thing which does not exist. I want you to think about everything you have seen. When I am ready, I will return to you and you will be required to make your choice. You will be given further particulars to help you make up your mind. For now, I bid you good night."

Archbishop Kraken slapped the roof of the pickup, and he and his guards sat down in the bed. The armed men kept the shotguns trained on the Phantom and the Nun.

The truck and the van turned around and drove off up the road.

"Well, that was interesting," the Phantom remarked, watching the vehicles disappear around a curve in the road. He turned to the Nun. "What were you about to say when we were interrupted?"

"Oh yes! I was sort of crawling around in the walls at the Cathedral Basilica downtown, and I happened to overhear a conversation. I was just sort of scuttling around, minding my own business, when I heard a voice I recognized. Archbishop Craig. I knew it right away because when Archbishop Craig was just Father Craig, he was my parish priest."

"Really?" The Phantom cocked his head and studied his odd interlocutor. "What is your real name? Can you even recall it?"

"No. It isn't important. Now, I respect the whole secret identity thing, you know, so I'm not going to draw any conclusions about who or what might be behind your mask. But Craig knows Joseph Perrone, who owns this house, and he thinks Perrone is the Bay Phantom. (At this point he winked, but it went unseen by the Phantom because of the porcelain mask.) And there's somebody named Kraken who lives in Craig's closet at the Cathedral Basilica. That must be the individual we just met. I heard them talking together, about Perrone and the Phantom. They are not in agreement about what to do. Kraken wants to kill you; Craig has some idea about making you useful or some such. That's why I'm here; I heard them planning this attack. The thing is, they have a whole organization behind them, I inferred that from the conversation I overheard. All of which ties in with what that character said just now."

"Well. That is something, all right. I appreciate your coming here to help, I really do. If you'd like to come inside, I think there are a number of things you and I ought to discuss, and—"

"I can't," said the Nun. "Not right now. I have things to do. Please just trust me right now. We'll talk soon. If you need me, call this number here and I'll come back to this house." He handed the Phantom a small business-sized card.

"Very well," said the Phantom, pocketing the pasteboard. "Thank you."

The Nun nodded, hopped into his roadster, and was gone.

Mirabelle opened the house, and she and Tom came out onto the porch to have a look at the prisoners.

Mirabelle performed a bit of triage on Forgone's ruined eye, then she and Tom tied him and the Mouse up with some clothesline.

"What do we do with them?" Tom asked the Phantom.

"I made a promise to a certain party, and I intend to keep it. We need to truss them up, and then, if you wouldn't mind helping me, Tom, we'll take them to a certain unoccupied house that I know of."

The Phantom picked up the phone and dialed a number.

"Lieutenant Matranga? Do you know who this is? Well, I made a promise to you, if you remember, and I just wanted to let you know that if you'll go to a house on the corner of Jackson and Congress streets in about an hour, you'll find two individuals that will interest you. I understand that the attack on police headquarters did not officially happen. I'm not making any recommendations, but, if you can't charge them with anything, you have an opportunity to deal with them as you see fit. I'm sure you'll do the right thing, whatever you perceive that to be. Oh, and one more thing, Lieutenant. Are you alone? You're sure? All right then. I thought you'd like to know that Tom Dart is alive, and he is under my protection... Yes, I am absolutely serious. Well, it's complicated, but I give you my word you'll get an explanation one day soon. Yes, you're very welcome."

The following morning, Joe Perrone paid a visit to the cathedral Basilica of the Immaculate Conception. He asked to see Archbishop Craig, but was informed that His Grace had left the Cathedral the day before, bound for the Vatican.

A quick swing by the St. Dymphna mission found the building shuttered and dark, with a sign tacked to the front door informing prospective recipients of charity that the premises were closed until further notice.

CHAPTER TWENTY-SIX

THE HOUSE ON THE EDGE OF THE WOODS

The girl's name was Carla English. Rickey Harvard had noticed her several times, in some of the markets and stores downtown. He'd first spotted her not long after that horrible Mardi Gras when he had nearly been eaten by his so-called friend Eddie Gein and the mad scientist Eddie had been working for.

Carla had dark brown hair, the exact same color as Coca-Cola when you poured it into a clear glass. Her green eyes made Rickey think of the green glass Coca-Cola bottles were made of, even though the shade was a little different, and her body was curvy, also like a Coke bottle. So she reminded him of Coca-Cola, which was why, not long after he first started thinking about her all the time, he quit drinking Orange Crushes and started on Coca-Cola.

Except the only thing he'd been able to afford to drink for the past few weeks was water out of taps, or the musty coffee they handed out down at the rescue mission, that tasted like they put dirt in it. In his mind, though, he was craving Coca-Cola. But that had all changed now, with the coming of the Suit. He could drink all the Coke he wanted.

Anyhow, he'd been hoping to see Carla again one day, and damn if he didn't run into her on the street right in front of the Battle House Hotel one evening. She was just walking along the sidewalk as he came out the door. He thought that was really something. It was just pure, blind chance. The same thing that had given him the gift of the suit. He was really on a roll!

He stepped in front of her and said, "Hey, do you remember me?"

She looked at him, and without bothering to try to recognize him, she said, "I don't think so."

"It's Rickey. Rickey Harvard."

"Oh," she said blankly. "Uh—Well, how are you? What have you been up to? You got a job?"

"Job? Heck, yeah! Say, how would you like to have dinner with me?"

"Well, I..."

"Would you like to go to the Silver Slipper? It's just on the other corner over there."

"Shoot yeah, I would. Not much chance of that happening, though."

"Oh, I don't know about that." Rickey reached into his pocket and withdrew a roll of bills. "I think maybe I might have enough." He thumbed through the tens, twenties, and fifties.

Carla's attitude seemed to change all of a sudden. It looked like she was prepared to tolerate him, though there didn't seem to be any real enthusiasm behind it. The green glass color in her eyes seemed a little bit warmer to Rickey, but he himself would admit that he had a vivid imagination. But he had made it this far, might as well keep at it.

"I guess that would be okay," she said, following the money with her eyes as Rickey returned it to his pocket. "I always wanted to eat there."

"Well, come on then!"

She was bored, he could tell. The suit and the money and the food and drink only went so far, he supposed. With a girl like this, you had to have something special. Lucky for him, he did. Maybe it didn't actually belong to him, but he had it, and that was what counted. He remembered his father saying once that possession was nine or ten cents of the law (when the old man had been in a dispute with a neighbor over the ownership of a shovel), and that seemed somehow to apply here.

They finished eating and Rickey called over one of the waiters he'd become acquainted with. He whispered a few words to the man, who smiled, winked, and scuttled off into the kitchen, reappearing a few moments later with a bottle of whiskey and two glasses.

"How about this?" Rickey said, after the waiter had gone. "Ain't this something?"

"Wow," Carla said. "Is that real whiskey?"

"Sure is," Rickey said, removing the cork from the bottle and pouring out two drinks. "They keep this stuff back for special customers like me. Go ahead, try it."

Carla picked up her glass and took a sip. "Oooh, that's pretty good. Almost as good as what Daddy makes."

Rickey gave the liquor time to do a little work on both of them before he spoke again:

"So, how's things been going with you, Carla?"

She made a face. "Oh, all right, I reckon—sort of."

"How come just sort of?"

"I don't like it out there," she said. "Where we live, I mean. I'd like to move into town, but Daddy won't hear of it. But it gets on my nerves, what with all the weird noises out in the woods and the spook lights and everything else."

"What do you mean?"

"Well, we been having some things going on. Some men have been trying to buy our place, Daddy's and mine. Daddy don't want to sell. He says his daddy owned the place, and his daddy's daddy before that, and so on and so forth. And he don't do nothing out there, just draws his pension check from when he got wounded in the Great War and makes his moonshine, and I reckon he thinks it's just the greatest thing that ever was. He says where would we go if he sold the place and I tell him we could move to town and he looks at me like I was crazy."

"Gosh. That don't seem right. But it can't be *too* bad out there, can it?"

"Well, then there's the spook lights."

"What's that? I never heard of that."

"Spook lights? Why, they're just these strange lights that float around out there. Spook lights. Lights made by spooks."

"Oh. Well, what else?"

"There's all the weird men. There's two kinds of them. I see them out in the woods a lot. One kind of them are the ones who go around in purple robes."

"Like bathrobes?"

"No, no. It's more like something out of the movies, like some kind of wizard or something would wear. They have big hoods on them that cover their faces."

"No fooling?"

A glimmer of an idea was beginning to take shape in Rickey's mind. They drank a little more of the whiskey, then Carla said she needed to be going. So it was now or never. Rickey readied himself as he escorted Carla out of the restaurant and offered to walk her to her car.

"Okay," she said. "It's parked right up the street."

They passed right in front of the Battle House Hotel, and Rickey stopped, grabbing Carla by the arm.

"I... I got something to show you, Carla. It's kind of a secret, so you gotta promise not to tell anybody."

She eyed him skeptically. "What's all this?" she asked.

"I want you to come with me. I got something I want to show you."

"Come where?"

"Up to my hotel room. Right here. Let's go in, huh? It's a swell room."

"I don't like this at all," she said. "I don't think I know you good enough. I don't think I ought to go with you."

"Aw, come on, Carla! I ain't gonna try nothing. You know I'm a gentleman. Didn't I buy you all those drinks? And a nice dinner? I got something real important I want you to see, honest!"

"This is how girls get into trouble," she said.

"Naw, Carla, it ain't like that," Rickey replied, growing a little desperate. This was his big chance to impress her, and she wasn't cooperating.

"Okay, look," he said, feeling a little frantic. "You don't have to go in anywhere. Just come around the corner with me, where it's private. I gotta show you something. See, I can maybe help you and your daddy. I mean with the spook lights and all that." He really had no clear idea what he was saying. How could he possibly help with a thing like that? But desperation was a reckless master.

"I don't know..."

He pulled her around the corner into a narrow space between the hotel and the next building.

"Well, just hang on a second and you'll see. Just stand right there, willya?"

"I guess, but you better not try anything funny."

"No, no of course not," Rickey said, slipping around behind a bunch of trash cans. "Now, don't look 'til I get ready to come out."

"You better not be taking your britches off back there."

...big hoods that cover their faces.

“Aw, don’t talk crazy,” he said, drawing the cloak out of the secret pouch in the jacket and fastening it around his shoulders. “You just wait a minute here, and you’ll be sorry for not trusting me more.” He yanked the mask and goggles out of the side pocket and hastily pulled them over his head. “Just one more second.” He adjusted the goggles, replaced the hat, and slipped his hand into the other jacket pocket for the final touch. Then, he stepped out from behind the trash cans, swirling the cloak with his left hand, brandishing the gleaming automatic in his right.

“Behold!” he said in a deep voice. “The Bay Phantom, at your service.”

Carla tittered. Then she giggled. Then she burst out laughing.

“What’s so darn funny?” Rickey demanded.

“You are! Where’d you get that silly outfit?”

“It ain’t silly!” he squalled, stamping his foot. “I’m the god dang Bay Phantom!”

“Oh, all right, if you say so.”

“It ain’t if I say so, it’s the truth. I can prove it too!”

“How are you gonna do that?”

“I’ll tell you how. I’ll go out with you and perform an investigation into them spook lights and things you was telling me about.”

Rickey hardly knew what he was saying at this point. There was no way he could investigate anything like that. But that might work in his favor. If she’d let him go out there with her, and he poked around and pretended to be making an investigation, she’d see how brave he was and how serious. There was nothing to those old spook light stories anyhow, so he didn’t have to worry about actually finding anything.

Carla rolled her eyes. “Well, if you want to, I reckon it would be all right.” She was feeling warm and a little silly from the whiskey. And then, too, there was the thing she hadn’t told him about. Maybe this was the right thing to do. “I’m parked just up the street, so come on, I’ll drive us out there.”

Louis Rickert stepped out of a little speakeasy on Royal Street. He had been drinking for the past couple of hours, trying to think up new places to go look for the Boss’ missing suit. He’d been to every pawn shop and used clothing store he could think of, with no results. He was only glad that Shorty Red was out of town so he could work in the problem in peace, on his own. Fortunately, the Boss hadn’t mentioned it to him yet.

As he hit the sidewalk, he saw something across the street and down the block that made him stop and stare.

It was the Boss, and he wasn't by himself. He was with a young girl Louis didn't recognize. Louis began to move in that direction to get a better look.

The two of them were walking up the street, away from the Battle House Hotel. A few people on the sidewalk stopped to stare as the Phantom walked by. Louis stared too, until they got a block or so away.

Louis started running. He crossed the street and dodged in between pedestrians, keeping the pair in sight.

That couldn't be the Boss, he thought. Too short for one thing. The girl was weaving a little, like she might be drunk, and so was the Bay Phantom, which was impossible. What the hell was going on here?

Then Louis smiled. So *that* was it.

Some bum had found the suit, and now he was parading around in it, probably trying to impress that dame. Well, this was a stroke of good luck, then. He could nab the guy and get the suit back before the Boss was any the wiser.

The fake Phantom and his girlfriend got into a little green car at the corner.

Louis flagged down a cab and jumped into the back seat.

"Follow that car," he said, pointing to the green car, which was just pulling away from the curb.

"Are you serious?" the driver asked. "This ain't a movie, pal."

"Come on, come on, hurry up! That little green car right there."

"Nothing doing."

Louis produced his pistol.

"Look, buddy," he said, "I'm sorry to do it this way, but I gotta follow them two. It's a matter of life and death."

"Awright, then," the driver said, putting the car in gear. "I guess you're the boss."

"I'll pay you later, honest, but please don't lose that car."

The car went left on Government Street, and then left again, onto the blacktop highway heading north.

Louis held the gun so the driver could see it in the mirror. "I swear, I ain't gonna shoot you," he said.

"Okay," the hackie replied, "but you realize you ain't making any sense, don't you? I mean, first you show a guy a gun to get him to do what you want, then you keep telling him you ain't going to shoot him. I'm playing along because I don't know what the hell you might do. But if you wanna make it as a crook, you should at least be consistent."

"Yeah, I'll keep that in mind. Just don't lose 'em, okay?"

Eliot Ness was about to get into his car at the side of the police station on Government Street, thinking about what a mess this damn town was, when he noticed something that caught his full attention. A car passed by on the street, its interior illuminated for a few seconds by a street lamp. It was driven by a young woman, but it was the man in the passenger seat that was the real object of interest. The Bay Phantom!

And right on that car's tail was a taxicab. In the back seat, Ness spotted a familiar face: Louis Rickert. Both cars took a left onto the highway.

Ness jumped into his own car, started the engine, and got behind the cab.

They went north, on past Chickasaw and into a semi-rural area that Louis was unfamiliar with. He made careful note of landmarks and whatever signs he happened to see.

They turned off on a little dirt road that ran in a straight line toward the woods. It was just another crummy country road, with lots of scrub bushes on both sides. They passed one house, close to the blacktop road, that had a telephone pole in front of it. A quarter mile further, there was a house that had an electric pole, but it didn't look like there was any phone hookup. The little green car pulled into the yard in front of it.

Louis told the driver to stop. They were far enough back that the fake Phantom and his girl wouldn't notice them, Louis hoped.

"You getting out way out here?"

"I said stop, didn't I?" Louis put his gun away and climbed out of the backseat.

"What do I do now?" the cabbie asked.

"Go back where you came from," Louis said testily. "See, I didn't shoot you, now did I? Here, take this." He thrust a pair of twenty-dollar bills into the driver's hand. "And don't tell nobody about any of this, okay?"

The cabbie gazed with amazement at the bills. "Hell, I guess you ain't no crook after all. What's the deal?"

"I'm a federal agent," Louis said. "Working undercover. My name's Ness. And you just done a service to your country."

"You shoulda said that to start with," the driver grumbled as he put the car in gear and cut the wheel to turn around.

Louis stood in the shadows, looking at the house, trying to come up with a plan. He could go in there, confront the punk with the suit, hold him at gunpoint if necessary, and make him drive back to Mobile in the little car. But he might have to corral the girl too, since she had been driving. Maybe the suit thief *couldn't* drive. And what if there were other people in the house?

He looked over at the woods beyond the house, when he noticed something. The only light out here had been the pale yellow one coming through the curtains at the front of the house, and the full moon, but now there were other lights, and they were moving!

They were coming out of the woods, over and through the dark trees—fireflies or something—*huge* ones.

No, those weren't fireflies. Those were more of the weird globes of light he'd seen whenever the strange, shambling men had appeared.

Some of those walking dead men might show up at any minute.

This was too much. He was in over his head, way out here in the middle of nowhere. Best not to let this get any further out of hand. He was just going to have to call the Boss and take whatever consequences were coming to him. There were times when circumstances forced Louis to behave sensibly, and this was one of them.

He walked back to the house with the telephone pole in front of it.

Thank God one of these hicks out here has a phone, Louis thought, mounting the steps to the porch and knocking on the door.

The man who answered struck Louis as an oddball. He couldn't say why, exactly, there was just something about him. He looked normal enough for this part of the world. He was about sixty, with a bald head, a long, horsey face, and big red hands, dressed in a work shirt and overalls. Louis couldn't quite figure out what was wrong about him. Something kind of fishy in his eyes, maybe. His right eye was focused on Louis, but his left one seemed lost in a world of its own.

"Can I do something for you?" the man asked.

Louis asked if he could use the telephone and offered to pay a dollar for the privilege. He felt kind of bad in retrospect about giving the cabbie forty whole bucks, but he felt he owed him something extra because of the gun. He wasn't planning on threatening this guy, though, so a buck was more than fair.

The man agreed and showed Louis down a narrow hallway to a telephone on a little table. The house was dark and close, and had a musty, sour smell that Louis associated with his grandmother's old country house. The phone was one of those old-fashioned candlestick types, so he had to fiddle with the hook and get the operator to connect him with the number he wanted.

He got the mysterious woman again, who handed him right over to the Boss. It was not until that moment that Louis realized he was going to have to give the Phantom a very awkward explanation.

"Uh, hello, Boss. This is Agent Rickert. Reason I'm calling is—You remember that suit you left up at my place, right?"

"Oh, yes. I've been meaning to come pick that up, but I've been a little preoccupied lately."

"Yeah, well, here's the thing, Boss. I, um, see, what happened was, uh—A burglar. Yeah, that's what it was. Some burglar must of got into the apartment while we was out and I guess he must of found the suit, because—"

"Louis—"

"But no, wait, listen. I've located it. I spotted the creep out on the street, wearing it, and I followed him. It wasn't easy, but I done it, Boss."

The Phantom sighed. "All right. So, did you retrieve the suit?"

"Not exactly, but I know where it's at. I'm calling from right nearby, I got eyes on the place. And there's one more thing. I saw some of them weird lights. You know, the ones that was swarming around when them rummies went nuts on Conti Street."

"Really?"

"Yeah. Look, if you'd like to come out and help me get the suit back from this punk—"

"Yes, yes, I suppose I'd better. Where are you?"

Louis gave him directions. The Phantom told him it would take about thirty minutes to get there, and instructed him to remain on watch.

Louis hung up, went to the small front room, thanked the man, gave him a dollar, and left. He was glad to get out of that dump, even though he was still out in the boondocks with no real idea what was going on.

Ness had lost the little convoy, but there weren't too many places that they could have gone. He had followed them for several miles north, outside the city limits and into what appeared to be the middle of nowhere. He lost sight of the two cars when they went around a curve, but there were just a few houses out here.

Ness checked two or three dirt roads that led off of the main black top before he hit paydirt.

He spotted the little green car parked in the front yard of a house that sat at the end of a short, rutted road.

There was no taxi here, but that was the car the Phantom had been riding in, he was sure. There was only one other house nearby that he had passed, closer to the blacktop road, and there were no cars in front of that one.

Ness parked behind a bush on the other side of the road and got out to watch the house. There was a light on inside. The dump was wired for electricity, but there was no phone line, like he'd seen at the house down the road.

He had only been waiting for about ten minutes when two figures stepped out onto the porch: the Bay Phantom and the girl he'd been riding with. What were they doing out here? Ness watched them as they walked away from the house and started for the woods.

Ness followed them down a narrow path through the trees. He didn't know what they were up to, but he didn't want them to get too far. He'd better just get this over with. He trotted along until he was just a few yards behind the pair.

"Hold it!" Ness barked, leveling his pistol at the Phantom. "Get your hands up, buddy!"

The girl let out a squeal and dashed off into the trees. Well, Ness would just have to let her go. He wasn't about to shoot her in the back. Anyhow, he had the big fish standing stock still in front of him.

"All right, Mister Bay Phantom," said Eliot Ness. "You just take it easy now. I'm not going to shoot you on sight, even though I could. I want to find out what you know."

Rickey swallowed hard and tried to say something. He wanted to tell this guy he had just found the suit and he wasn't the Bay Phantom, but he couldn't find any words. And it didn't really matter, since they wouldn't have been able to make it past the lump in his throat anyhow.

"Keep your hands up," Ness said, "and don't try anything funny. You and me are going to take a trip downtown. If you even look like you're going to pull any stunts, I'll drill you, get it?"

Rickey's knees wobbled and his stomach started making dire noises.

That was all the response he could manage. Ness stepped over and pulled his arms down behind his back, snapping a pair of handcuffs onto his wrists. Then he marched the hapless faux Phantom back up the path, across the road, and into the back seat of his automobile.

Louis Rickert had walked back to his original position just in time to see Ness arrive. Oh cripes, *him* again! What was he doing way out here? He ducked behind a bush to see what was going to happen.

Ness got out of his car and watched the house for a little while. When the fake Phantom and the girl came out and started off into the woods, the fed followed them.

A minute later, Ness came back out, leading the guy in the Phantom suit by the arm. Louis watched as Ness shoved the faux Phantom into the backseat of his car and went around to the driver's door to get in.

Terrific, just terrific.

He watched Ness turn around and drive off toward the blacktop road.

Well, shit, what do I do now?

He stood and looked at the house. Beyond it was nothing but dark woods. Louis didn't like the woods. He was more at home in the city. Too many trees got him disoriented, they all looked the same.

The weird lights were gone, but they could come back at any time.

He thought about what he had just seen. The only people who had come back out of the woods had been Ness and the other guy. The girl hadn't been with them. So she was still out there. She might know something. Louis decided to venture into the woods to try and find her. There was a chance he could still come up with something to give to the Boss. If he could catch her and bring her back without anything happening, that might appease the Boss a little bit over the whole suit business.

He wouldn't push it, though. He'd look for a few minutes, and if he didn't find her, he'd come back to the rendezvous point to meet the Phantom.

CHAPTER TWENTY-SEVEN
THE CASTLE

"Louis said he'd meet us here," the Phantom said. "This is the house."

"Well, then, I'm not surprised he isn't here," Mirabelle said. "He's probably passed out drunk out in those woods somewhere."

The Phantom had pulled his sedan up in front of the home of Carla English and her father. Louis Rickert was nowhere to be seen.

"Now, Mirabelle, Louis has cut down considerably on his drinking. I know you have a poor opinion of him, but he can be relied on—up to a point. I'm afraid something has happened to him."

"If you really plan on keeping him, you ought to put him in one of the cages with your mice."

"He said he spotted the suit he, ah, lost, and he also saw some of those floating lights out here. That's why I wanted you to come with me. You might get some idea of what they are. I just have a feeling everything that's been going on lately is tied together. After all, I believe he and Shorty were targeted that night. If we can find out who took the suit—"

"Rickert probably pawned it," Mirabelle said. "And those lights he says he saw probably came out of a bottle."

"Oh, Mirabelle. Louis can be exasperating, but he has a good heart."

"So do a lot of people who are total screw-ups. It's no reason to keep indulging him."

They got out of the sedan, and mounted three rickety wooden steps to the porch of the house. The Phantom knocked on the door. It was answered by an elderly man in work pants and a flannel shirt. He had a round head topped by a thatch of yellowish hair, a lined face, and small blue eyes filled with suspicion.

"Here *you* are again," the old man said, "and now you got a *colored* gal with you! If that don't beat all. What did you do with my Carla?"

"Sir, I have never been here before, and I don't know who your Carla is. But if there's a problem of some kind, I'd like to help sort it out."

The old man studied him for a moment.

"Yeah," he said, scratching his chin, "you don't seem like the same fellow that was here before. I reckon you might be the real McCoy. This fellow I mentioned come in here with my girl, Carla. They acted like they was friends. He said he was here to make some kinda investigation out in the woods. We been seeing some peculiar things out there. Strange lights and odd-looking men and such. He acted like he didn't have half-sense, to tell you the truth. It looks like somebody might be dressing up like you and messing with young girls."

"That will never do," the Phantom said. "If your daughter is in danger, I assure you I'll do everything I can to bring her back to you safely."

The man went to the edge of the porch and pointed off to the side of the house.

"I reckon they went down that little trail yonder. It leads off into the woods. Carla wouldn't of got lost, she's been running around out there her whole life. I'm afraid that feller took her off down there and done something to her."

"I hope that's not the case," said the Phantom.

He and Mirabelle set off down the trail, picking their way along with the beam of a small flashlight. There were several sets of tracks plainly visible, two of them belonging to men, one to a woman, judging by the shoe prints.

"Look, Mirabelle. Both sets of men's shoe prints come and go. They must have returned from some point up ahead. But the girl wasn't with them when they came back. See here, the girl went this way and did not return. At least she was by herself, nobody dragged or carried her away."

They followed the small footprints for a while longer, until they veered off into the underbrush.

"Well, damn," Mirabelle said.

The Phantom held up a hand. "Just a moment." he craned his neck, peering out into to dark woods. Then he raised the flashlight and illuminated a small figure standing next to a tree.

"Miss, are you all right?" he asked.

"Oh, no, not you again!" the girl exclaimed, shrinking back.

"I believe you encountered someone else, masquerading as me," the Phantom said gently. "I assure you, Miss, that I am the real Bay Phantom."

Carla moved a bit closer, studying the Phantom and Mirabelle in the moonlight.

"Yeah, I believe you might be," she said. "Your voice sounds different. And you're taller too."

"Indeed. Do you know anything about the man who came out here with you?"

"Oh, it was just some idiot boy I met. Ronny Something-Or-Other. I guess he dressed up like you to impress me. He wanted to get into my panties something awful."

The Phantom started coughing and Mirabelle slapped him on the back a few times. "Steady, there, Boss," she said.

"And what happened to him?" the Phantom asked after he had regained his composure.

"Some guy took him away at gunpoint. The guy talked like he was a cop."

"What did he look like?"

Carla gave him a quick but surprisingly detailed description. The Phantom leaned over to Mirabelle and whispered, "Eliot Ness."

"Anyhow," Carla went on, "I thought that dumb ol' Ronny might really be you and could maybe help us figure out what's been going on in these woods, you know?"

"If this has been going on for some time, why didn't you go to the police?"

Carla waved a hand dismissively. "Aw, it ain't nothing for the police. Plus which, my daddy runs a little still, so we don't need the law poking around our house. But I never heard of the Bay Phantom messing with any moonshiners. We don't hurt nobody."

"I'm sure you don't. As you say, I'm not interested in your father's activities, but I am very interested in these 'spook lights.' You've seen them?"

Carla nodded. "Oh, sure. Lots of times. Sometimes they're close to the house, but they're usually way out in the woods. They seem to like to hang around the old castle."

The Phantom and Mirabelle looked at one another.

"Castle?" the Phantom said.

Carla nodded again. "Yeah, the old castle in the woods. It's been out there for a while, I don't know how long. I never saw it until a couple of years ago, which seems funny, since I been living out here my whole life. But it looks real old. Nobody ever goes there. Nobody but the dead men and the men in robes."

"The dead men, eh? I think I know what you mean by that, but who are the men in robes?"

"Well, I reckon they could be women. You can't really tell with those big purple robes they wear."

"I see. And what do these people do?"

"Nothing I can make any sense out of. They just wander around in the woods, especially over near the castle. And one time I saw three or four of them leading a whole bunch of those dead men, like they was a little herd of cows. Looked like they was taking them to the castle."

"Can you tell us how to get to this castle?" the Phantom asked.

"I can take you there if you'd like. Close enough to see it, anyhow. I don't like to get too near to it."

The area they entered consisted of acres and acres of untouched woodland. Hundreds of square miles, actually. They walked for perhaps a mile and a quarter from the English house before they came to a large clearing in the woods, a bowl-shaped depression, perhaps a hundred yards in diameter. In the center of it stood a most remarkable building.

At first glance, it might have been a replica of the Cathedral Basilica of the Immaculate Conception in downtown Mobile—until one began to notice the subtle differences. Even in the moonlight, it didn't take long to spot them. For example, the imposing columns out front weren't fluted; they were scaled, like serpents. The crosses atop the two towers were inverted.

"Look," Carla said, pointing. "Just like I told you. Spook lights."

Sure enough, dozens of small, glowing orbs swarmed around in the air above the building.

"Spook lights," the Phantom repeated. "Charles Fort used to write about them. He had no firm idea what they were; he considered everything from earthbound spirits to vehicles from other planets."

"Well," Mirabelle said, "I don't know that we need to go that far afield. But I have to say, they don't look like any of the more conventional suspects. They aren't ball lightning or St. Elmo's Fire, and they damn sure aren't lightning bugs. I would cautiously suggest some kind of electromagnetic phenomenon, either natural or manmade."

"That's very vague and general, Mirabelle. It isn't like you to hedge your bets so comprehensively."

"I know. But here we are."

"Indeed."

Mirabelle studied the place for a few moments, growing uneasy as she did so. "Something's going on in there," she said in a whisper. "I don't like to say things like this, but it just feels *weird* out here."

"Can you quantify that?" the Phantom asked.

"Of course I can't," Mirabelle said. "And you can't tell me you don't feel it too. Listen for a second and tell me what you hear."

"Nothing."

"Exactly. Where are the crickets and all the other night noises? Whenever this happens in novels, it isn't good."

"Kraken is there," the Phantom said. "Don't ask me how I know that.

And he was right. He said the only way I'd ever find him was by pure, blind chance. I don't know what else you'd call this."

"I don't wanna stay here," Carla whispered. "Have y'all seen enough?"

"We'd better take Miss Carla here back home," said the Phantom, "and go and get some reinforcements. Miss Carla, is there anything else you can think of? Anything odd that you may have seen or heard, especially within the last few days?"

"Well—No, nooo, nothing like that."

"Come now, you were going to say something. What was it?"

"It's silly."

"Tell me anyhow. We won't laugh at you, I promise."

"I—Well, sir, there were some ghosts in the house, all right? Just last night. Never had no ghosts before."

"Really? What did they look like?"

"I didn't see them. I heard them, talking to me. Whispery voices, sort of fading in and out, like the radio at night."

"And what did they say?"

"They sort of didn't make sense. They said some things I didn't understand, about chances and being blind and I don't know what all. Then they told me to be at a certain place at a certain time. So, I—I did it, I went where they said, when they said. And that was where I met up with that stupid boy who pretended to be you."

"Are you all right?" the Phantom asked Mirabelle. He had noticed that his friend was looking unwell all of a sudden. From the expression on her face, she might have been punched in the stomach."

"Yeah. yeah, I'm fine. Let's get moving, okay?"

They accompanied Carla back to her house and restored her to her father, who thanked them profusely and offered them a jug of moonshine for their trouble. The Phantom politely declined, but when he headed back to his sedan, Mirabelle hung behind and surreptitiously accepted the offering. She had a feeling she might need it later, if she made it through the coming night.

"Winona knows how to fight," Mirabelle said, as she drove the sedan back toward Tull House. "And she's healthy enough now. I just have a feeling we should bring her."

"Right," the Phantom agreed. "And I'd like to bring the Emb—the *Nun* along too. In fact, I need to make a call. He gave me a number and said to phone him if we needed his help. He'll meet us at Tull House if he's available."

"Good Lord, why?"

"You have your feeling about Winona, and I have mine about the Nun. If you explain yours, I'll explain mine."

"I can't," Mirabelle grumbled back.

The Phantom removed his hat to don a pair of headphones, and used the radio in his car to patch into the telephone network via an electrical relay back at Tull House. Speaking into a hand microphone, he gave the operator the number. It rang four times and a man answered.

It was a voice the Phantom recognized, but it was not the Embalmer. It was Paul Darcy.

He cut his eyes over at Mirabelle. She was concentrating on the road.

"Uh, yes," he said, "this is the Bay Phantom. A gentleman who gave me this number said he could be available if needed."

"Oh, hello, Mister Phantom. It's nice to hear from you. I've been feeling a lot better and I've been wanting to thank you for getting me away from that Klan bunch. You know who this is, right?"

"Yes, and you're quite welcome. I must say, you sound well, and I'm gratified. I'd like to talk to you some more in the future, but we've got quite a situation going on just now, and we need some help. If you could convey the message—?"

"I sure will. He just stepped out to get some tea. I'll let him know as soon as he gets back. Oh, and listen, sir—I may be way off base here, but I need to ask you something. Do you know a Mirabelle Darcy?"

"As a matter of fact, I do. You remember, then."

"Yes, sir. How is she doing? Is she all right?"

"I can assure you that she is. We'll talk more about that later."

"Okay, and thank you. Thank you so much. I'll give him your message soon as he gets back. You take care, now."

The Phantom ended the call and replaced the headset and microphone.

"Who was that?" Mirabelle asked. "Don't tell me he's got a secretary?"

"He stepped out to get some tea," the Phantom said, evading the question. "Curious thing, isn't it?"

"Tea? I'll be damned. You don't think about a psychopathic lunatic going out to buy tea."

"No, that's true, you don't," the Phantom agreed. "I wonder what kind of tea he likes."

"Who was that you were talking to?"

"I prefer green tea myself. I think it's much healthier than the other kinds."

"So you're going to ignore my question, then? Okay, suit yourself. Talk about tea some more. Anyhow, I'm not dumb. I know who that was."

"You do?"

"Uh-huh. Your tone of voice changes when you get nervous. He's got that damn Penny Carter holed up with him, doesn't he?"

"I'd rather not say," the Phantom replied, greatly if temporarily relived.

"Oh, I'll bet," said Mirabelle.

"I believe we have found our adversaries' home base," the Phantom told the assembled company back at Tull House. "I propose that we mount an expedition there, immediately."

"Yes, I want to go with you," Winona said. "I think maybe I need to."

"I have no objections," said the Phantom. "I don't know what we're going to find out there, and you are certainly a formidable presence."

"Are you sure you're okay?" Mirabelle asked her.

Winona nodded.

"All right then," said Mirabelle. "It could be dangerous. Probably will be. I've got a sword you could use, if you'd like."

"Why not? For old times' sake. But I'll take a gun too, if you don't mind."

"Well, *I'm* ready," Tom Dart said. "I can't wait to get my hands on those—"

"No, Tom," the Phantom said firmly. "I want you to stay here with your family. You have escaped death once already, there's no sense pushing it. If I don't make it back, I'd like you to take care of things here. I drew up some papers the other day. They are in a safe in my bedroom. The key is in here." He handed him an envelope.

"No, listen, I can hel—"

"I'm sorry, Tom," the Phantom interrupted him, "but I must insist on this. For one thing, from the way Kraken talked the other night, I don't believe he and his cartel know that you're still alive. I would prefer to keep it that way. And there are other considerations. I know you're willing to risk your life to help a friend, but this isn't about you and me. Think of Maizie and Coral. If I should die tonight, I'll go easier knowing I didn't deprive them of you for a second time. You know I'm right about this."

Tom just nodded.

"If I fail to return within in reasonable time," the Phantom continued, "and you do not hear from me, have Maizie take the deeds down to city hall. They will make her the new owner of Tull House and all of its secrets. You will find details in a journal in the safe. You may feel free to use the available resources to accomplish the clearing of your name and your return to life. There are a couple of possible courses of action that Mirabelle came up with—you'll find those in the safe as well. The details will be up to you, but I'm sure you're equal to the challenge.

"Unfortunately, Joe Perrone's banking accounts will probably be tied up in probate until such time as he can be legally declared dead—Maizie will be the executor of his estate, but there will be hoops to jump through—however, you will find a considerable quantity of cash and negotiable bonds in the bottom of the safe."

"I don't know what to say," Tom told him. He struggled to keep his facial expression neutral, and swallowed a couple of times in an attempt to dissolve the lump that was forming in his throat.

"I know. I wouldn't either. This is an extraordinary situation, Tom. I hope none of this will be necessary, but only a fool fails to take precautions." The Phantom laid a hand on Tom's shoulder and said, "Thank you for everything, my friend. These are, as I say, merely precautions. I'm sure we'll meet again very soon."

"We'd better," Tom said in a near-whisper. "We had damn well better." He was doing a good job of keeping his face under control, but he could do nothing about the tears that began to run down his cheeks.

Mirabelle led Winona upstairs to a large closet she used to store some of her belongings. She rummaged around for a few seconds, until she found what she was looking for.

"Here it is," she said, lifting a scabbard with a sword in it. "This belonged to my father. I had forgotten about it until... someone reminded me the other day. Strange thing for a man like him to have. He used to say it was made out of 'ghost metal,' whatever the hell that means. Looks like plain

"I'm sure we'll meet again very soon."

old steel to me. Somebody traded it to him for one of his home remedies, he said." She laughed. "Evil people aren't supposed to be able to see it."

She handed it to Winona, who drew the blade out of the scabbard.

"*I* can see it," Winona wryly observed, staring at the sword. She ran her thumb very lightly along the edge, then sheathed the blade and strapped the scabbard to her back. "It feels like it doesn't weigh anything at all," she said.

Mirabelle bit her lip and said, "Come on, let's get you a gun to go along with that."

"I'm glad to see you looking well," The Nun said to Mirabelle, after the Phantom had introduced them down in the front room. The madman had arrived while Mirabelle had been upstairs with Winona. "We had us a hell of a time at that Donner-Purdy Funeral Home back in February, didn't we? What do you think of the new outfit?"

"This is beyond anything I've ever seen," she said to him, shaking her head. "What made you decide to—? Never mind, I don't want to know."

"Are you sure? It's a dramatic origin story, and very inspiring too, if I do say so myself."

"No."

"Suit yourself. There is an element of blind chance in it that might almost be termed Shakespearean."

Mirabelle almost asked him about that remark, but decided to leave it alone.

They returned to the woods in the Phantom's sedan, parking across the road from the English house, and setting off down the path once again. Winona was silent, while the Nun kept up a running stream of inane and irrelevant chatter. The Phantom ignored this, though Mirabelle was growing steadily more irritated.

"You know," the Nun said at one point, "this kind of reminds me of an episode of *Myrt and Marge* I listened to the other day. I mean, there were no woods, and it was daytime, and it was really nothing like this situation at all, but it just had a similar, I don't know, *je ne sais quoi* to it."

"Oh, for God's sake," Mirabelle said. "Can you please keep that shit to yourself?"

"Not a *Myrt and Marge* fan, eh? Well, I'm the first to admit that they're not for everyone. You strike me more as the *Little Orphan Annie* type."

"You're damn lucky you didn't say *Amos and Andy*."

"Please be quiet, you two," the Phantom interceded. "We need to keep our ears open."

They reached the clearing and stood for a few moments, gazing at the bizarre building.

"All it needs is bats," Mirabelle remarked.

At that moment, a small flock of them burst from the window at the top of the right-hand tower and fluttered untidily across the dim face of the moon.

"Well, there you are," said the Phantom. "And not just bats. Look."

He pointed to a spot in the sky above the towers.

"The spook lights," Mirabelle whispered. They studied the small globes meandering about over the weird cathedral. "There are more of them now, aren't there? What the hell *are* those damn things?"

"That's the question," said the Phantom.

They stood at the edge of the clearing for twenty minutes, watchful for any further signs of life—signs of *human* life. There were none. The bizarre structure remained dark and quiet.

They began to skirt the edge of the clearing, treading carefully, and when they reached a certain point; they noticed something at the opposite edge, beyond the building.

"Look at all those cars," Mirabelle said. There were at least a dozen of them, parked along the opposite tree line, all expensive-looking.

"Hmmm. It appears someone is hosting a gathering. They've come in from the other side there. What's over that way, Mirabelle, do you know?"

"Nothing to speak of. About seven miles to the north there's the main road between Satsuma and Mauvilla. It cuts right through more woods. This forest continues west on over to the Mississippi state line."

"Well, here we are," the Phantom said. "There's nothing to be gained from hanging back. Are you all ready?"

Winona nodded. The Nun said, "I've no other plans." Mirabelle said, "You know I'm with you."

Moving carefully, they descended the slight slope into the depression. The monstrous "cathedral" seemed to swell before them as they approached.

They walked around the thing once, twice, Mirabelle examining the wall and other features with the aid of her small flashlight.

"This is not recent," Mirabelle said. "This thing has been here for a long time."

"How long, do you think?" the Phantom asked.

She shook her head. "No way to be precise. I'm gonna say fifty years at least. Based on several observable factors, and leaving a margin for error of twenty years both ways. *Thirty* years. But, yeah, it's not new."

"Hm. Possibly eighty years old. If so, it might have been constructed around the same time as the actual Cathedral downtown."

"Maybe. Depending on how long it took to build this—thing. The real Cathedral was begun in 1835, and it was completed in 1850."

"Hm. Miss Carla said she wasn't sure how long *this* has been here. She never saw it until fairly recently, though. Curious. How could a thing like this escape notice, even in such a remote location, for such a long time?"

Winona stared at the building, the look on her face suggesting that she was seeing more than just a stone structure. Her eyes were unfocused, as though she were looking inward rather than outward.

"It's not here," she said softly. "It doesn't exist, not really, not in the way we think of the concept."

Mirabelle moved to her side.

"Are you okay, Winona?" she asked.

Winona nodded. "Yeah, Mirabelle." She put out a hand and touched the wall in front of her. "This thing is beyond existence. I can't explain it, but I know."

"She's right," the Nun said. "I can feel it too. This thing has never been here, but it has always been here. It's part of the Cathedral Basilica downtown, but not really. I have a unique relationship with the original building, and I can feel a kinship to this one as well."

"If that gobbledygook is the best you can come up with," Mirabelle began, irritated both by her companions' cryptic remarks and the disturbingly unscientific nature of the situation, but she was interrupted before she could finish her complaint.

"So you found us," came a cold voice from behind them. They turned slowly.

There were fourteen individuals standing there, all dressed in long, dark robes, with voluminous hoods that concealed their faces. Two of them were armed with shotguns.

"You folks need to drop your weapons and come with us," one of them said.

They glanced at one another. "I suppose we've no choice," said the Phantom. They complied, with one exception: Winona left the sword where it was, in the scabbard strapped to her back. The robed characters seemed not to notice, or they didn't care. It was a curious oversight, but none of the Phantom's party said anything, of course. Winona herself, whose unnatural calm could almost be described as beatific, seemed to take it as a matter of course.

The four were marched at gunpoint around to the front of the building, up the uneven steps, and on into the "cathedral." Immediately inside the doors, they took a left turn into a corridor lit by smoldering torches sent into sconces along the walls, at the end of which was a cell with a barred door. One of the robed men opened it with a large, old-fashioned key.

"Get in there," he said. "The Archbishop will be along to see you momentarily."

They filed into the small room. All four walls were of flat, gray stone, as was the floor. Three benches were attached to the walls, and they all sat. The door was closed and locked behind them. Dim illumination came through a small, barred window in the door.

"This is nice," remarked the Nun, swiveling his head around. "Very monastic. Ascetic, I might say."

"Shut up," Mirabelle muttered.

They remained there for almost thirty minutes. The Phantom tried the door and decided that there wouldn't be any point in trying to breach it. He could probably manage it, but they would surely be caught immediately.

It was almost midnight when one of the robed men returned and unlocked the cell. He was accompanied by two of his fellows, both of whom carried shotguns.

"Come on," he said. "We're taking you to see the Archbishop. He's making preparations in the sanctuary and can't come here."

The little group was led out of the cell, back up the corridor, and into the "sanctuary." The mock "nave" was a nightmare, rows of pews occupied by what looked—and smelled—like human corpses.

The whole place was lit by torches stuck in sconces around the walls, dozens of them.

Where the altar should have been was a shallow pit some twenty feet in diameter. In the center of this was a slab of what appeared to be dark marble, with several iron rings bolted onto the sides.

Standing behind the slab was a man in a purple robe, wearing a mitre adorned with a skull and crossbones. It wasn't Kraken, though. It wasn't the man who had visited Tull House. The Phantom recognized him, though.

Archbishop Craig.

CHAPTER TWENTY-EIGHT

A WASTE OF TIME?

When Ness called in to say he had picked up the Bay Phantom, Lieutenant Matranga had a few bad moments. Was it possible? Ness wasn't a superman, after all. How had he managed to pick up the Phantom all by himself?

Matranga had brought the Scarecrow and the Mouse back to headquarters the night before and locked them up. They were charged with trespassing and having no visible means of support. Foregone had somehow sustained a rather gruesome eye injury, which had received some treatment already, and might receive a little more by and by. Neither of them had talked to anybody about anything, and they didn't seem particularly worried. They went to their cells with the air of men who expected to hear from a lawyer at any minute.

Matranga hadn't mentioned the Bay Phantom to Ness or anyone else, and neither had the two prisoners. If Ness had really managed to apprehend the masked man, a huge can of worms might be on the verge of opening up.

Matranga watched nervously as Ness brought the masked man into the booking area. The first thing the on-duty personnel did was remove the hat, mask and goggles.

"Well," said one of the cops, "who the hell is he?"

"Who is he?" another one said. "This ugly little zero is the terror of the underworld!"

Matranga studied the face that had been revealed. The guy couldn't be more than nineteen or twenty. His face was soft and pasty-looking, and a look of terrified astonishment seemed permanently stamped on his features.

He looked as though he might have sense enough to pour piss out of a boot, but not much more. *If this is the Bay Phantom*, Matranga thought, *I'm Amelia Earhart.*

The young man was processed through the booking department, where he was relieved of all his property, and issued a gray jumpsuit to change into.

For more than an hour, the young fellow was too terrified to utter a word. He finally managed to communicate to one of the officers his desire for a bottle of Coca-Cola. Matranga okayed it. When he had finished half of the soft drink, he found his voice, and gave the officers his name, Rickey Levon Harvard. A quick check revealed that he had no prior arrests.

He was taken to one of the small interrogation rooms, where he was put further at ease with another Coke and a ham sandwich. One of the detectives started the questioning, and Ness and Matranga watched through a two-way glass from the next room.

The interview started off rocky, and went downhill from there. Rickey Harvard was cooperative enough, and he grew more comfortable and less agitated as things progressed. But it soon became apparent that he didn't know much of anything, and probably wasn't playing with a full deck to begin with.

"This punk ain't the Bay Phantom," Matranga opined.

"Of course he's not," Ness agreed. "But he knows *something*. That gun he was carrying is the same caliber as the one that put that bullet into the Mouse, and I'll bet ballistics will find a match. And then there's that suit. He didn't buy that stuff in a costume shop."

"Well, let's see what he has to say."

They went into the interrogation room and took over from the detective who'd been talking with Rickey. Before he left, the detective pointed to his temple and twirled his finger around. "Good luck with this character," he muttered.

"All right, kid," said Ness. "Rickey, is that right? Rickey, where did you get that outfit? And that gun?"

"I done told you guys I don't know how many times," Rickey said around a mouthful of ham sandwich, "I found it in an alley downtown." He swallowed meat and bread and washed it down with what remained in the little six-ounce bottle of Coke. "Somebody must of throwed it out a window or something. I was just walking along and poom! There it was. Say, you reckon I could have another Coke?"

"Sure, sure. Now, tell us what you were doing out at that house where I picked you up."

Rickey gave them a rather confused account of his dealings with Carla English. He confided that he had pretended to be the Bay Phantom in order to impress the girl, but said he hadn't meant any harm by it. He repeated once again the story of how he found the suit.

"Okay," said Matranga, "but exactly *where* did you find it? Could you show us?"

Rickey shrugged. "I dunno, I might could. I ain't sure which way I was walking, I was kinda shook up. It was downtown somewheres, I know that."

"Well, you think about it," Matranga said. "You ready for that Coke now?"

Rickey thought for a moment. "Y'know what?" he said. "Do you reckon I could get an Orange Crush instead?"

Ness and Matranga stepped out into the hallway.

"We aren't gonna learn anything from that idiot," Matranga said.

"Don't I know it," said Ness. "I think I might have better luck out there where I picked him up. Maybe I could get something out of that girl he was with. She must have lived in that house I saw them coming out of. He said the girl talked about 'spook lights.' You said there were some weird lights here in the building when Foregone came in and busted the Mouse out."

"That ain't much of a connection," Matranga said.

"You got a better one?"

Matranga had to admit that he did not.

CHAPTER TWENTY-NINE

MIDNIGHT IN HELL'S CATHEDRAL

"You," the Bay Phantom said.

Craig nodded and smiled. It wasn't a sinister smile, but one of genuine welcome and tentative hope. "I was going to come and get you, Joseph," he said, "when we were finished with our work here tonight. I can't imagine how you managed to make your way here on your own, but I suspect it was a stray wisp of my own will that brought you. That is encouraging. I have been arguing with Kraken over your fate. He sees no value in your continued existence, while I see you as a valuable potential ally. And, of course, I am somewhat sentimental, and cannot simply ignore our long association. Not that I will hesitate to destroy you if you cannot be convinced, of course. Do not mistake my kindness for weakness."

"Oh, of course not," Mirabelle said. "I can tell you're a regular humanitarian."

"Miss Mirabelle Darcy," Craig said, nodding his head and sounding pleased. "I was hoping I'd get a chance to meet you. From what Joseph has told me, you are a most remarkable young lady. I understand that the attitude of society at large toward those of your race has been a vexation to you. I assure you that you will find no such prejudices here."

"Terrific," Mirabelle said sourly. "So I have to join some kind of Edgar Allan Poe freak show to be accepted. That's life for you."

Craig smiled. "You have a sense of humor. That will take some getting used to." He addressed himself to the robed minions. "These two are important," he said, pointing out the Phantom and Mirabelle. "The others are not. Take them over by the doorway, just there." He gestured to a spot on the wall outside the pit. Winona and the Nun were marched over there and made to stand with their backs to the wall, guarded by two robed men with shotguns.

"Well, then," said the Phantom, "now that you have us here, there must be something you want to do."

"He wants to tell us about his master plan," Mirabelle said. "They always do. It's a psychological compulsion. I'm thinking of writing a paper on it."

"Actually, Joseph, she's right," Craig said, sounding much like the kindly priest he had once seemed to be. "I do want to tell you about my own life, in hopes that you will understand my position and perhaps discover some common ground."

"Well," the Phantom said, "I suppose I've nothing else to do this evening."

"That is quite true," Craig agreed. "And, as for what you have to do with the remainder of your life; that will be up to you, once you hear what I have to say."

"Fair enough," said the Phantom. "Please proceed."

"Thank you. After I was ordained as a priest, but before I took up my duties in Mobile, I traveled to the Vatican. After my visit there, I toured Europe and England. When I was in London, I met Aleister Crowley and learned of his philosophies. I had heard of him and done some reading. What I had learned about him intrigued me.

"Not surprisingly, I was always keenly interested in the concepts of good and evil, and the various forms each of them took. Quite naturally, I became curious about the 'wickedest man in the world.' When I was young, I saw things in terms of black and white. But as I learned more about Crowley and the systems he dabbled in, I began to perceive some fascinating shades of gray. For me, the Church had always represented absolute good, and any who opposed its teachings absolute evil. What I learned from studying Crowley disturbed this absolute conviction of mine, and I had to know more. I knew I must meet him, and I managed to arrange it.

"At the time, he was the leader of the British branch of the Ordo Templi Orientis, and he was propounding his Thelemite beliefs. I obtained an introduction, and when he learned that I had come not to denounce him, but to subject him to some relatively open-minded questioning, I believe he became as intrigued by me as I was by him.

"We ended up spending a week together. Crowley is hardly the monster he has been portrayed in the popular press, but he is extremely unconventional. I was not terribly interested in the sexual aspects of his beliefs, but certain other ideas of his found fertile ground in my mind.

"I returned to Mobile and took up my duties as a parish priest.

"It was after I had been here for a while—a year, perhaps, maybe two—that I met Kraken. He had ideas similar to my own, but he took them much further. I have never been a terribly imaginative man, Joseph, but Kraken—Well, he seems to know no boundaries.

"Before long, I abandoned my primitive ideas about good and evil, God and the Devil, for good and all.

"Together, Kraken and I established the Anti-Diocese of Mobile. We conceived the idea of the Anti-Diocese as a mechanism for working our will upon the world. With Kraken's unique powers of discernment, it was easy for us to find individuals who could be persuaded to share our aims, to add their wills to ours.

"I rose in prominence in the Church, until I was finally ordained as Archbishop a year ago. It was only fitting that, at the same time, Kraken was ordained as Archbishop of the Anti-Diocese of Mobile.

"It has been an interesting partnership. We disagree on certain particulars, as is to be expected, but together we have built an organization to be proud of. And it is based upon the real truth, the only truth about the organizing power of this universe.

"The *will*, Joseph, the *human will* is the basis of all magick, all occult beliefs and systems. Conventional religion exists solely to subvert that will, to drain it off into foolish faith and subservience to an illusion.

"You may be familiar with one of Crowley's maxims, 'Do as thou wilt, that shall be the whole of the law.' But it means more than you might think. It is not an exhortation to irresponsible hedonism, it is a *formula*. Yes, a formula for nothing less than complete control of *life itself*.

"This building we're standing in did not exist on this spot until a few years ago; and yet, it has existed since the original Cathedral Basilica of the Immaculate Conception was constructed. *My will brought it here!* It is a shadow, you see, just as Kraken is my shadow. And you have a shadow too, Joseph. You wear it. And you have one too, Miss Mirabelle."

"I'll bet she's a fat white girl," Mirabelle remarked.

Kraken ignored her and continued his monologue.

"Faith is a drug for fools. The only thing one can trust is one's own will. Join me, Joseph. You know what it means to rise above the merely human. You've done as I have. *We* are the gods, Joseph. There are no others. There is nothing out there but darkness, silence, cold. No God, no Devil. Only us."

"I cannot accept that," said the Phantom. "I won't."

"That doesn't change the facts."

"No, but I will not assume any facts that aren't in evidence."

"Oh, really? Isn't that what you've done your whole life?"

Behind his mask, the Phantom smiled. "You believe you can win this conflict with sophistry? You really don't understand me at all. You're right, I do have faith. Faith in myself, but only insofar as I serve something higher than myself. And faith in my friends."

"Tell me something, then. When you decided you wanted to oppose criminals, why didn't you become a policeman? Or an attorney? Do you even know? Because I do. You became the Bay Phantom because you know, you feel, that the rules and structures created by others are not for you. You became the Bay Phantom because that's what you are. It is your *will*."

"It's just a mask, that's all."

"Is it? Is it really? Or is it something else? Is it a clumsy attempt to do what I have done?"

"And exactly what is it that you have done?"

"I'll show you. You will see. It is time for you to meet Kraken—to really *meet* him. Then you will see. I will summon him for you now."

Craig stared at the Phantom and something extraordinary happened to the once-kindly old priest. The skin of his face seemed to shrink until it was pulled taut over the skull beneath. At the same time, it changed color, going from pasty white to sickly purple. The pupils and irises of his eyes faded out until his eyes were blank yellow orbs.

"Now, do you see?" he said, his voice a hoarse croak. "This is not a mask. Kraken is not a thing that Craig puts on and takes off."

"Very well," said the Phantom, seemingly unperturbed by what he had just seen, "but what do you intend to *do*? What is the purpose of all this? Do you mind enlightening me on that score?"

Kraken smiled. It was not pleasant; it looked like a grave medical condition of some kind.

"Excuse me!" the Nun called out from where he stood against the wall with Winona. "I think *I* might be able to provide a little enlightenment here."

Kraken swiveled his head in the Nun's direction. "You will be silent," he said. "I have only allowed you to live this long as a concession to Joseph, who seems to hold you in some esteem."

"I think it might behoove you to listen to what he has to say," the Phantom told him. "I'd like to hear it myself. It might help me to make a decision."

Kraken was silent for several moments, staring at the Phantom. "All right," he said. "I will indulge you." He gestured to the cultists. "Bring that... *thing* over here."

The Nun was escorted down into the pit.

"What is it that you feel the need to say?" Kraken asked.

"Well, the thing is, you see, I might be—at least in part—responsible for this whole thing."

"What? What do you mean by that, exactly?"

"When I was younger, I had a friend who encouraged my interest in exotic chemical experiments of various kinds. This was when we were both schoolboys, and Father Craig was our parish priest.

"We both read *The Strange Case of Doctor Jekyll and Mister Hyde*, and developed a bit of an obsession with it. The idea of a formula that could turn a 'good' man into an 'evil' one occupied our thoughts and conversations, and, quite naturally, this obsession began to inform our independent experimentation.

"My friend was quite brilliant, and I was not without a certain amount of talent myself, if I may say so. Consulting a number of texts of a rather unusual nature which my friend had obtained, we created what we believed to be Doctor Jekyll's original formula, or something very close to it.

"Being mere boys, we tended to see the world in black and white terms. Any priest, to our immature minds, was automatically 'good.' Father Craig came to symbolize that condition.

"We kept an eye on him for several weeks after that, administering further doses of our potion. As we observed no change in the Father, we figured our efforts had come to nothing, and we moved on to other pursuits."

"How in the world did you manage to convince yourself you could duplicate that formula?" the Phantom asked.

"Well, I read *The Strange Case of Doctor Jekyll and Mister Hyde* four times, right in a row."

"There is nothing in that book that details any of the components of the formula."

"I was reading between the lines."

The Phantom shook his head, for want of any better response to such a statement.

"This cannot be," Kraken said. "If you are telling the truth at all, which I very much doubt, your puerile 'formula' had nothing to do with me. Craig and I are not two sides of some metaphysical coin, and I certainly do not owe my existence to such childish piddling as you have described. I suspect that Joseph has coached you, or that you have taken it upon yourself to attempt to confuse me. If this is what you must resort to, then your position is hopeless indeed.

"Take this creature back to the wall. It may prove useful yet, once I have convinced Joseph here of the rightness of what I am saying. If that proves impossible, then it shall be killed along with the other one."

"I should have known I'd have trouble with pronouns when I put this outfit on," the Nun grumbled, as he was led back to stand next to Winona.

"Now," Kraken said, rubbing his hands together, "where was I before this bit of absurdity intruded?"

"I think you were about to explain your ultimate purpose," the Phantom said helpfully. "Or some such thing."

"Yes indeed, thank you. You asked me what I intended to do. Well the answer is very simple: We of the Anti-Diocese of Mobile are going to lift the city up and out of this plane of existence!"

"Oh, well, then," Mirabelle said.

"Allow me to explain. We have constructed a device. We call it a bomb, though it isn't an explosive in the traditional sense. The mechanism is based on principles advanced by Professor Einstein. Imagine several tons of TNT detonated all at once. And more than that! Not merely the initial explosion, which will be like nothing the world has ever seen before, but wave upon wave of deadly radiation. Indeed, the radioactivity will poison the land for decades to come."

"Can they do that, Mirabelle?" the Phantom asked.

"You're asking me?" she said. "I don't know, Joe. I doubt it, but—*Theoretically*, rupturing or splitting the right kind of atom *could* produce a tremendous release of energy. But it would have to have an atomic number of 94, at least, and no such thing exists now."

"That is correct," said Kraken. "But it will, and soon. All we need is the proper radioactive element to achieve fission. We will use the energy of our wills to transform a—*base metal*, if you will, ordinary radium—into a new element. This very night in fact. One I call *satanium*. We have made some preliminary attempts to convert radium. Those murders that have so concerned you were, as you may have surmised, occult rituals. There is power in such ceremony, you know, and our friends from Chicago were enthusiastic participants.

"But we were not ambitious enough. Tonight, that will change. We have sacrifices enough here tonight to generate sufficient energy—our 'zombies.' We have hundreds of them now, all of them in the cellar beneath this cathedral. Their slaughter, together with the climate of fear we have generated in the city, will allow us to achieve our objective."

"That is the silliest, most nonsensically convoluted thing I have ever heard," said Mirabelle. "Aside from the fact that your premise is complete bullshit, there's not even any internal logic to this so-called plan of yours. I think you've just been playing around. I think you're insane. And now that we've found you, you've come up with this dramatic foolishness to frighten us or to amuse yourself, I don't know which. You're sick."

"I suppose our activities must appear so to the uninitiated. But if you knew what I know, if you understood what I understand—"

"You're full of shit," she declared, "that's all there is to understand."

"Why, Miss Mirabelle, there is a place here for you as well. Race and sex are meaningless distinctions. Only fools use them as a basis for judgment. You're obviously quite brilliant; you show a more than passing familiarity with Professor Einstein's work."

Mirabelle snickered. "As a matter of fact, I know Professor Einstein. And you're no Einstein."

Kraken scowled at her and was about to make a reply when he was interrupted by a voice from the front doorway.

"Archbishop, we've caught another interloper outside."

Two more robed figures approached the edge of the pit, holding Eliot Ness by the arms between them.

"Yet another minion, Joseph?"

"I do not have *minions*, Kraken. That is where you and I differ. I have *friends*."

"And this man is a friend?"

"I have never met him, but I think it's safe to assume that he and I are on the same side—at least in theory."

"The *losing* side," Kraken sneered. "Put him there with the others."

The robed minions led Ness over to the wall where Winona and the Nun stood.

Kraken said, "It looks as though Providence is attempting to lend you a hand—rather ineptly, however."

"I thought you didn't believe in anything."

Kraken shook his head. "You're not listening, Joseph. I believe in power, in forces that are created by, and can be commanded by, *man*. That is what the so-called occult is: Man tapping his own limitless potential. The tools he uses to do this are imagination and allegory. That is what I mean when I rather ironically say 'Providence.' The Devil is nothing but primeval matter and energy and the forces that move and manipulate them, the same as God. Obviously, your own desires led you to find me, and have attracted another of your *friends* here. That's fine. My will, and the will of the Anti-Diocese, is superior to yours. Do you believe that?"

"If you say so," the Phantom replied. "But that doesn't explain what you intend to do with this bomb of yours."

Kraken nodded. "It must be puzzling to you. Of course, setting it off way out here wouldn't accomplish much. No, we're going to transport it downtown and install it in the Cathedral. You remember the renovation work Craig showed you on the sanctuary, to which you so generously contributed funds? It will go there. A place has been prepared in one of the upper stories. A rather fitting place, and centrally located to do maximum damage to the city. Everyone within, oh, a half-mile radius, give or take, will be killed outright, and there will be ancillary deaths for some time to come."

"That's your ambition? What will it accomplish?"

"I told you. It will lift the city out of our reality. I don't expect you to understand, not now. I am giving you one last, precious opportunity to understand. Will you take it, Joseph?"

"Whatever poor powers of persuasion you believe you possess," said the Phantom, "they are lost on me."

"I will beg if I must." Kraken knelt down on the stone at the Phantom's feet. "Join us, Joseph. Please."

And the Bay Phantom looked down and whispered, "No."

Kraken turned to Mirabelle. "And you?"

Her reply was extremely vulgar, even by her usual standards.

"Very well, then," Kraken said sourly. "The choice was always yours. Your annoying steadfastness has been your undoing."

He rose smoothly to his feet. "Bind them," he said, "Bind them to the slab. Joseph, you and Miss Mirabelle can still be useful, as sacrifices."

Four of the robed cultists seized Mirabelle and the Phantom and bore them down onto the slab. Two lengths of rope were produced, and they were bound securely, the cultists passing the ropes through the metal rings at the sides of the slab and knotting them tightly.

"Tell me this, Kraken," the Phantom said. "If you don't believe in anything, to whom are we being sacrificed?"

"Why—To *me*, Joseph. Who else?"

A line of shambling men emerged from the doorway and gathered around the slab. They were accompanied by a swarm of the weird "fireflies," bobbing and circling in the air above their heads. At a command from Kraken, they all lay down on the stone floor.

"We will kill them, and you. The resulting death energies, coupled with my will, shall convert the uranium into satanium."

Mirabelle started laughing uncontrollably.

Kraken moved to her side and produced a long-bladed knife from within his robe.

"You won't be laughing when I put this through your heart, Miss Mirabelle."

She got herself under control and said, "Well, no shit! Of course I won't!"

He raised the knife...

Louis Rickert was lost.

He had been wandering through the woods for what seemed like hours. It couldn't have been very long, though, because the moon hadn't moved very much. He knew that much about the sky, but he didn't know anything about how to find your way out of the goddamn woods when you were lost in them. He examined several trees, but couldn't find moss on any of them. He remembered hearing that moss grew on the north or the south sides of trees, and that was somehow supposed to be helpful. But there was no moss anyhow, and the moon was just sitting up there, not telling him which way to go.

So he kept walking, until he reached a clearing. It dipped down from the tree line, forming a shallow bowl, in the middle of which stood a huge building. It was sort of like a church, Louis reckoned, but it looked more like some kind of spook house. Some of those damned floating globes of light were meandering around in the air over the top of it.

Whatever this was, Louis wanted no part of it. He walked along the edge of the clearing, hoping to be able to see some sign of civilization on the other side of this monstrosity. If not, he'd just have to try to go back the way he came and take his chances. He kept following the edge of the tree line, his eyes roaming over the weird building. Then he saw something which filled him with relief.

There, around one side of the building was the Boss, and he wasn't alone. There were three women with him. Two of them looked kind of familiar, and the third was a nun, of all things.

Louis had been about to yell a greeting to them when a bunch of guys in purple robes appeared and pointed guns at the Boss and the three women. They were led around to the front of the building, up the steps, and inside.

Louis trotted down into the clearing, swiveling his head back and forth the entire time, on the lookout for more weirdos in robes with guns. None appeared.

He walked all the way around the building, gun drawn, but there didn't appear to be any other entrances. At the rear, on the opposite side to where the steps were, he found a vague rectangle in the bare wall, a little darker than the surrounding stone, about the size and shape of a doorway. Was it a secret entrance? He got closer. It was difficult to examine it in just the moonlight, but he thought he could see a very thin crack running between the darker and lighter sections. He pressed at the center of the rectangle, and thought he felt it give, ever so slightly.

He pushed harder, and the whole thing swung inward. It *was* a door! It was a secret door and he had found it! His excitement overcame his fear. Now he had a chance to make good. He could rescue the Boss and those ladies, and the whole thing with the suit would be forgotten.

The corridor in which he found himself was dark, but there was a bit

It was a secret door!

of light coming through the doorway. He advanced until the light was so far behind him that he was in complete darkness. The floor sloped sharply downward, and he groped over to the wall, keeping his left hand against it as he continued on, gripping his pistol in his right. Fear was beginning to reassert itself, and he did his best to ignore it, pretending that he was in his own apartment, drunk, trying to find the bathroom.

From somewhere ahead of him, he heard a humming noise. It grew louder as he advanced, and he gradually became aware of a dim, purple light somewhere ahead of him. The faint illumination made it easier to move along the corridor, until; finally he was just a few feet from a doorway. The light was coming from the room beyond. He inched toward it, sweating like crazy, until he was close enough to peek inside.

It was a large chamber, with walls, floor and ceiling made of gray stone.

Close to one wall, several people in purple robes were fussing around a huge machine of some kind. Louis had no idea what it might be. It looked like an enormous water tank, with dials and gauges all over it, and pipes that led off into the floor and one of the walls.

Against the wall next to it were stacks of what looked like lead bars. Several of the robed characters were busy lifting them from the stacks and carrying them off through an arched doorway at the far end of the chamber.

Louis thought, or tried to, but he didn't have a lot to work with. He didn't know what this big machine was, but it seemed important to the jokers in the robes, and they were the bad guys. Therefore, maybe if Louis were to somehow sabotage the machine, that would be a good thing. He wasn't sure exactly how to go about it, or even if he should, but the only other course of action was to sneak back out of the building and go home, and that didn't seem like the right thing to do.

Well—He *did* have a gun. He could shoot the machine, whatever it was, and put it out of commission. If it belonged to bad guys, it must be doing something bad.

Okay, then. Shoot the machine. That was the plan. He dismissed from his mind any thought of negative consequences that might arise from this course of action. He had to do *something*, and this was it.

He stepped gingerly around the doorframe and into the room. He raised his pistol, his hand trembling only slightly, and took aim at the weird machine.

"Hold it right there. And drop that pistol."

The voice had come from behind him. He slowly turned his head and saw one of the robed goons pointing a shotgun at his midsection.

"Aw, Jeez," Louis said. He dropped his gun.

"Archbishop, we've caught another one." A robed cultist stood in a narrow doorway to the left of where the chancel would have been in a proper cathedral. He motioned with a hand and through the doorway, arms gripped by two more cultists, came Louis Rickert. They brought him to the edge of the pit.

Kraken lowered the knife and looked down at the Phantom. "Well. You have a never-ending stream of these flunkies, do you not?"

"Sorry, Boss," Louis said sadly. "I was gonna try to get you out of here, but they nabbed me."

"I'm sure you did your best, Louis."

"Another *friend*, eh?" Kraken said, cocking his head and studying Louis. "Well, Mister Bay Phantom, I'm going to show you now just how much your *friends* are worth. Bring that trash down here."

"Trash?" Louis repeated indignantly, as he was dragged up to the slab where the Phantom and Mirabelle lay bound. The cultists held him there, in front of Kraken.

"Enough of this foolishness," Kraken said. "Let us get on with our business here." He raised his hand.

A number of the robed figures congregated in the area around the pit.

Several others emerged from the doorway that Louis had been brought through, carrying in lumps of gray metal, stacking them in what would have been the chancel, had this been a church.

"We have quite a quantity of uranium here, as you can see," Kraken said. "Our smaller scale efforts to convert it came to nothing, but we are assured of success tonight."

"This is madness, Craig," the Phantom said, not unkindly. "You need help. Give this up and let me do something for you. I can get you treatment. Given time, you could—"

"No, no. You won't turn this around that way. You are the one who needs help, and you have refused it. So be it." He turned to the cultists who had gathered in the pit. "You might as well show them who we are, so they will know, in the end, what they were up against. None of them will be leaving here alive." He waved a hand at the robed figures standing nearest to the slab. "You three,' he said. "Show them."

Three of the cultists stepped forward and pulled back the concealing hoods. The Phantom and Mirabelle recognized them immediately.

Chief Prater.

Mayor Gordon Armstadt.

District Attorney Cumber.

"I assure you, the rest of our number are equally prominent," Kraken said. "These are *my* 'friends,' if you will. As for yours—"

He stepped closer to Louis, examining him in the torchlight. Louis kept his eyes cast down toward the floor.

"I think this fellow's will is not so formidable." He reached out a hand and touched Louis lightly on the chin. "Look at me."

Louis looked up into the ghastly face.

"What is your name?" Kraken asked him. "Louis something. Louis what?"

Louis didn't want to say, but he couldn't help himself. "Louis Rickert."

"Yes, of course, Louis Rickert, the flawed angel. You can be useful to your master when it is in your best interest, but you are essentially a selfish little creature."

"Who, me?"

"Yes, you," he said. "You aren't really much of a man, are you, Louis Rickert? I can see into you, you know. Yes. You are venal and timid. You are a schemer. Always out for yourself."

"That ain't true," Louis said stubbornly.

"You profess loyalty to the Bay Phantom, but that is only because he rewards you. He pays you money and he flatters you. But you are not loyal, not really."

"Like hell I'm not!"

"Yes indeed. Like hell. I have something for you, Louis." Kraken handed the long-bladed knife to Louis.

"So what the hell am I supposed to do with this?" he asked.

"Oh, nothing very much, Louis," Kraken said. "Only do as I tell you." He pointed at the Phantom. "Kill your boss."

"Aw, no," Louis said, shaking his head. "Never."

"Yes, you will," Kraken gently insisted, laying a spidery gray hand lightly on Louis' shoulder. "Look at me, Louis. Look into my eyes."

Louis obeyed, almost involuntarily. Kraken's eyes seemed to swell and to protrude slightly from their sockets. Louis could not look away from them.

"Kill your boss," Kraken repeated.

Louis felt the weight of the knife in his hand; it seemed like it weighed a hundred pounds. He knew he had to do what this guy was telling him to do. He couldn't do it, but he had to. He didn't want to, but he had no choice.

He was in the grip of something he didn't understand, and he had no wiggle room at all. *Oh, what am I gonna do now? I* have *to do what this mug says, and I—wait a minute—*

He thought about it. What did the word "boss" mean, anyhow? Somebody you worked for, of course. When your boss told you to do something, you had to do it.

So... That made this weirdo in the robe Louis' boss right now, didn't it?

"Go on now," the man said. "Do it."

"Let's just make sure we're clear here," Louis said. "Do what?"

"Kill your boss!"

"You *sure* that's what you want me to do?"

"*Yes*!"

Louis nodded. "All right, *Boss*, you asked for it."

He plunged the knife into the robed man's stomach. Then he quickly pulled it back out and used it to slash the ropes that held the Bay Phantom and Mirabelle.

Kraken had toppled over backwards, gravely injured if not dead. Several of the cultists had rushed to him. The others seemed not to know what to do, and stood stunned, looking this way and that.

"Thank you, Louis," the Phantom said, helping Mirabelle off the slab. "That was extremely well done."

"Aw, thanks, Bo—uh, *Phantom*. I think I better watch what I call you for the next little while, just in case." He handed the knife to the masked man.

The Phantom turned his head to Mirabelle. In spite of the mask and goggles, she knew just what sort of a look he was giving her.

"All right, all right," she said. She sounded a little testy, but she was smiling, and she went so far as to pat Louis on the shoulder.

The Phantom leapt over the prone "zombies" and into the circle of people surrounding the slab, fought his way through them, dealing out several bone-shattering blows in the process, and disarming several gunmen. He reached Eliot Ness, Winona Dirge, and the Nun. Using the knife Kraken had intended for him, he freed them.

"This is not over yet," he said, handing them the pistols he had procured. "Help me subdue as many of these characters as we can. No need to be gentle about it, I suppose."

Mirabelle and Louis had already waded into combat with the cultists. Before joining them, the Nun tugged at the Phantom's sleeve.

"Listen," he whispered, "if I don't make it out of here, and you do, there's a fellow I've been sort of looking after." He reached into the habit and produced a small card. "This is the address where he is. Take care of him, won't you?"

"I will, and I thank you. You're... the best person you can be, I think."

"You too, pal. Now, let's do some damage!"

Two of the cultists had gone to Kraken and pulled him into a sitting position, though he was motionless and might have been dead. The knife protruded from his midsection.

His eyes opened. He grasped the knife by the hilt and drew it out of his body. He looked at it for a moment. The blade was stained with some kind of thick, black ooze. His shoulders shook slightly, as though he were chuckling, and he tossed the knife away.

Kraken waved away the cultists who had clustered around him and rose to his feet.

"Well, that stung a bit," he said. The front of his robe was stained black, but he did not appear to be bleeding. "You see now what my will can do. But that isn't the end of it, no. Watch this."

Kraken swelled to almost twice his normal size, stretching the seams of his robe, which now only reached halfway to his knees. Absurdly, it reminded Mirabelle of a flapper, and she almost giggled. But his skin had turned a deep red, and he now sported a pair of small horns on his forehead, and that was not amusing at all.

The Phantom, the Nun, and Eliot Ness all fired at Kraken, with no visible effect. The cultists all stood motionless, shoulder-to-shoulder, forming a human barricade between their leader and the Phantom's party. They did nothing to prevent the gunfire, but it seemed that they didn't need to. The bullets seemed to vanish before they could strike the Archbishop.

Ignoring the volley, Kraken crouched down like a spider and stretched out a hand toward the pile of uranium. The metal began to glow, then to shimmer. It seemed to melt and flow up in an arc toward Kraken's hand. When it touched his fingertips it produced a shower of sparks. Kraken screamed as the wave of liquid metal flowed into his hand, and he grew larger still, absorbing the uranium until all of it had disappeared.

"You see how hopeless it is! He crowed. "You can do nothing. I *am* the satanium! Look at me, Miss Mirabelle, my body is now a living reaction chamber. The energy I contain is beyond comprehension! I can do *anything*! My will is supreme, and my will is to crush you all. I am all the Devil that there is, and all the God too. *There is nothing else out there!!!*"

He straightened and drew himself up to his full height, which was nearly twenty feet at this point.

"No," came a voice from back near the wall. "You're wrong, Kraken. There *is* something out there. I know. I've been there and come back."

Winona Dirge.

"You're wrong, Kraken," she said. "Dead wrong. Let me show you." She moved forward. A number of the robed cultists stepped into her path.

"Stand aside," Kraken said to his minions. "Let her approach. There is nothing to fear."

"You think that," said Winona. "I've got something for you."

The cultists stood down and Winona advanced toward Kraken.

"Winona!" Mirabelle shouted. "Don't! I can't just let you—"

"Mirabelle," Winona said, briefly glancing back at her friend. "Thanks for everything. You know how we talked about me never giving it to somebody who deserved it? Well, this is my chance. I can do it. You're not going to mess it up, are you?"

Mirabelle grimaced, her eyes filling with tears. "No. No, goddammit, Winona, I won't."

"You're a good friend."

Am I? Mirabelle wondered as she watched.

Winona strode forward with no apparent concern over the monster she was approaching. With one hand, she drew, from the scabbard at her back, the sword that Kraken's minions had inexplicably failed to take from her.

Tentacles sprouted from Kraken's back, four of them, flailing in the air like streamers in the wind. One of them whipped around and swung toward Winona. She stood still and raised the sword Mirabelle had given her. Just before the tentacle could come into contact with her, Winona swung the sword and lopped off about four feet of it. Kraken emitted a strange chattering noise that might have signified pain or might have been hysterical laughter.

Winona kept up her offensive, whacking away with the strange sword. She cut off half of another tentacle, and slashed at the remaining two until they dropped to the floor and lay motionless. She came to within a foot of Kraken and smashed him across the side of the head with the flat of the sword. He made a noise like air leaking from a tire and fell over onto his side.

It was far from over, Winona knew. Kraken was down, but only momentarily. He would be back up again very soon. She stepped back a foot or so and hefted her blade, waiting for the monster to rise again. Doubt suddenly assailed her. Kraken was stirring already. Winona raised the sword, prepared to bring the sharp edge down onto Kraken's exposed neck.

She swung.

The blade hit Kraken just below the base of the skull, with a harsh metal-on-metal sound, striking sparks. The blow had failed to even break the skin.

"Oh, no," Winona breathed.

"Let me by," said the Nun. He fought his way through the cultists, who were busy with the Phantom, Mirabelle, and the others, until he reached Winona's side.

"I can help," he said.

Winona looked at him quizzically. "Do I—Do I know you?"

"I think so," said the Nun. "I'm not sure, but—" he reached up and tore off his mask.

Winona stared at him blankly for two seconds before something dawned in her eyes. "Why—it's *you*."

"Right. It *is* me! I remember now. And you're Winona! Now that I remember you, darling, I wonder how I ever could have forgotten! I had such a crush on you, and it has not diminished a whit while it languished in the oubliette of my subconscious. My first and only love!"

"Oh, I missed you too," Winona said, her eyes brimming with tears.

"Well, I *told* you we'd meet again. I just didn't know it would be so close to the end."

The Nun stretched out a hand to Winona and she took it.

Kraken suddenly bellowed, reared up, and grabbed both of them, one in each hand, and lifted them up off of the floor as he rose to his full height, which had almost doubled since he fell. He tried to pull them apart, but could not.

Winona began hacking with her sword at the hand that clutched her. The fingers twitched and split and bled a black ichor, but held on. So Winona started working her way up the arm, cutting huge gouges into the purple flesh. Black liquid flowed from them like lava from cracks in the earth.

The Nun, meanwhile, had been whacking away at Kraken's other hand with his ruler. This seemed to be having more of an effect than one might expect, all things considered. The ruler, like Winona's sword, was opening great rents in Kraken's flesh, and the monster's black "blood" was pouring out of them.

As much damage as the pair was inflicting, however, it seemed to be a race against time, as Kraken's hands were inching toward his open mouth. His intention was quite clear, and it seemed unlikely that Winona and the Nun could sever his hands before he was able to swallow them.

"Winona, I have just the thing," the Nun exclaimed.

The Nun tossed the ruler away and reached down into the bodice of his habit, pulling out a large Saint Christopher medal. He touched a small stud on the side of it, and a tiny light began to blink. He stuffed the medallion into Kraken's mouth, plunging his arm in all the way to the elbow, and held it there.

The Nun shouted, "Grant me, O Lord, a steady hand and watchful eye, that no one shall be hurt as I pass by—except for *this* thing, of course! So long, Winona! So long, Phantom! It was—"

His final words were cut off by a terrific explosion. Whatever the Saint Christopher medal had been packed with had detonated like a land mine. Winona and the Nun vanished in a flash of orange light, and Kraken's body split in half, right down the middle. From the monster's core, a bright red light blossomed.

The light grew brighter. The building shook. Cultists screamed and staggered around in circles, bumping into one another. The light slowly flowed out from where Kraken had stood, engulfing the cultists one by one.

The Phantom, Mirabelle, Louis, and Eliot Ness made for the front doors. They got through and ran until they had ascended the slight slope and reached the tree line. Then they turned to look back at the building. The Phantom was reminded of the biblical story of Lot's wife.

But there was no building.

There was just a column of blood-red light. The Phantom, Mirabelle, Louis, and Eliot Ness just stood and stared. No one said anything because there was nothing they could have said. There were no questions they could ask one another that could possibly be answered, no observations they could offer that would make any sense at all. So they stared.

The light throbbed and twisted, causing the trees in the surrounding woods to cast wild shadows. Hundreds of the weird "fireflies" swarmed around the column, until they started winking out, one by one, until none were left. Then the red light contracted to a narrow beam.

And then there was nothing.

Nothing but a clearing in the woods.

"What do you think happened here?" Mirabelle wanted to know.

"I think Father Craig learned a lesson," the Phantom said. "Or Archbishop Kraken, or whatever you wish to call him. I don't suppose it matters much now."

"What you call him doesn't matter, but what happened does."

"That's what I meant. What do you think happened?"

She shrugged. "I'm just gonna have to fall back on what Hamlet said to Horatio. I know that whatever we saw was possible because it happened, but I don't know what it was, because I didn't create this universe. I just live here and try to figure out what little I can."

The Phantom placed a gloved hand on her shoulder.

"Poor Winona," she said. "I hope she's... I don't know, Joe, what *do* I hope?"

The Phantom shook his head. "Just say you hope she's at peace, Mirabelle. That's what people say, isn't it?"

"I guess so."

"Well, I choose to believe that she is. I wish her soul the best, and I honor her. The Embalmer too."

"Well, let's not push it."

"You may soon have reason to revise your opinion of him."

"What the hell do you mean by that?"

The Phantom said nothing. Uncharacteristically, Mirabelle did not press him.

Twelve hours later, there was nothing to be found in that clearing. Not a brick, not a beam, not a blade of grass. Nothing but a large patch of lightly charred vegetation and the corpses of some twenty crocodiles—animals which are not indigenous to North America. No human remains were discovered by the small band of searchers.

"I suppose," the Bay Phantom said to Mirabelle Darcy, as the sun neared its zenith, "that if you had anything like an explanation for this, you'd have voiced it before now."

"You suppose right. Please never ask me about this again, because you know how much I hate to admit that I just plain damn don't and can't and never will understand a thing."

"Agreed."

"Good Jesus, what the hell happened out here?" Eliot Ness asked, pushing his hat to the back of his head and wiping his brow with a handkerchief. He and Louis had been searching the woods around the clearing for any sign of anything. Their search had, of course, been fruitless.

"I wish I could answer your question, Mister Ness," said the Bay Phantom. "I was just discussing that very thing with Mirabelle."

"I was thinking," Ness said, "that maybe there was some kind of hallucinogenic gas or something in that place that made us imagine we saw—what we saw. And they were talking about making some kind of exotic explosive in there. Maybe they had some and it got set off, and that's what destroyed the building."

"Right," Mirabelle said. "A hallucinogen that made us all imagine the exact same thing, and then an explosive that vaporized the whole building but didn't harm the ground it was standing on—and filled in the hole to boot. There was a cellar in that place, remember. Now there's no sign of it. I'm afraid *exotic* doesn't quite cover that, Mister Ness."

"No, I suppose it doesn't. However, when I write my report, which I'm going to have to do, that is what I'm going to suggest. Not *assert*, only suggest."

"And what will your report assert—or suggest—about me?" the Phantom asked.

Ness smiled. "It will say that you are a masked vigilante whose identity remains unknown. It will say that I was unable to learn anything about you or any of your associates, but that you were instrumental in overturning a particularly nefarious conspiracy. Those cars parked over there will tell us something about the people who were here last night. My report will assert or suggest that no efforts should be made by federal authorities to curtail your activities."

The Phantom nodded. "I appreciate that, sir. I think I may still be of use to the people here in my current condition."

"You're okay," Eliot Ness told the Phantom. "I can't exactly say I approve of what you do, but I guess my approval, or lack of same, isn't an issue. I can see that you deal with things that I can't even—" He shook his head. "Well, I've always believed in the principle of the right man for the job, and as far as this town goes, it looks like you're him."

"I suppose so," the Phantom said.

"Tell me something. Doesn't that mask ever get uncomfortable?"

"To tell you the truth, I hardly even notice it any more."

Ness just nodded.

CHAPTER THIRTY

AFTERMATH

With the death—or disappearance—of Craig/Kraken, the combine known as the Anti-Diocese of Mobile swiftly fell apart. Most of the prominent members died or disappeared—or something—in the destruction of the anti-cathedral.

A number of prominent people, many of them high up in city government, had simply vanished. Investigations into their private and business lives would uncover irregularities that would take years to untangle.

Kraken may have been mad, but at least a few of his cultists had more method to their activities. A consortium that included the mayor, the police chief, several city council members, and others had recently sold large tracts of land in Mobile, at grossly inflated prices, with promises of future developments and substantial profits for the buyers. Of course, the records of these insider transactions—along with the buyers themselves—would have been destroyed in the explosion. In fact, the paperwork on all manner of double-dealings would have been vaporized, and the cultists would have enjoyed their profits in locations far away from Mobile.

As for the Scarecrow and the Mouse—It happened that they were still wanted in Chicago, according to information provided by Shorty Red, so the pair were held only until they could be extradited. Prosecuting them for the crimes they had committed in Mobile would have been messy and overly complicated. Back in Chicago, both would face multiple homicide charges, and, following their trials and swift convictions, would die in the electric chair at Stateville Correctional Center in Crest Hill, Illinois, on February 17, 1933.

Lieutenant Carl Matranga would be among the witnesses.

Eliot Ness would go on to other investigations and adventures. In 1935, he would become public safety director of the city of Cleveland, Ohio. Though he would accomplish much in his new job, his tenure would be best remembered for his failure to catch a brutal serial murderer known as the Mad Butcher of Kingsbury Run. The case would bring back memories of Archbishop Kraken's bloody reign in Mobile, and fact that the killer would manage to elude the law would haunt him until the end of his days. Ness' personal life would be marred by an unsuccessful run for mayor of Cleveland, two divorces, and serious financial difficulties.

His continuing fame would be assured by a book he would co-write with Oscar Fraley. *The Untouchables*, a rather sensationalized account of his work in Chicago during the Capone era, would become a best seller and be the basis for a popular television program. Unfortunately, Ness' renewed celebrity would be posthumous. Ness would die of a heart attack on May 16, 1957, shortly before the publication of his memoir.

"Tom will be all right," Gladys told Perrone one morning, a week after the disappearance of the Anti-Cathedral. "And the Phantom has been cleared too. Matranga was keeping files. All kinds of evidence against the people who did this to Tom, stuff he didn't know if he could ever use, but he kept it, and kept collecting it. I'm not saying Matranga's conduct was above reproach, sitting on all this, but he was scared and he didn't know who he could trust with it."

Perrone nodded. He and Gladys were sitting at a table out in front of a sidewalk cafe on Dauphin Street.

"I can't blame him," Perrone said. "He was terribly hemmed-in. I'm just thankful he assembled the material he did. He's a good man, Gladys."

"Yeah, I suppose he is," Gladys agreed. "He just needs plenty of prodding and support to show it. As it is now, he's going to be working with Eliot

Ness and some other federal agents to investigate everything.

"Anyhow, what with all that's happened, Tom's conviction and death sentence will be overturned, no doubt about it. And as far as his escape is concerned—the prevailing view at City Hall, as expressed by our new mayor and police chief, seems to be the less said and the fewer questions asked, the better."

"I suppose it will be not only safe, but also expedient, for Tom to come out of hiding soon."

"Oh, yeah. Not only won't they file any more charges against him, they'll probably make *him* chief."

Perrone smiled and shook his head. "Tom tells me he has no intention of returning to the police force. He wants to set himself up in business as a private detective. Quite a good idea, I think. And I believe the Bay Phantom can provide him with some remunerative business until he can build up his own clientele. We can't have Maizie and Coral starving, after all."

One cloudy afternoon a few weeks later, Tom Dart paid a visit to a small cemetery in Prichard. He and his family had emerged from the bowels of Tull House and returned to their little house. Tom had gone through everything he had to endure with the authorities, and come out of it with his record and reputation absolutely clean.

A graveside service was in progress when he arrived at the cemetery, and he joined the small group of black mourners, who gave him strange looks but said nothing. He was sure they were wondering why a white man was intruding on their grief, but they did not voice their curiosity.

He stood watching as the plain wooden coffin was lowered into the grave.

After the service was done and a couple of men had started shoveling dirt back into the hole, the mourners filed out of the cemetery, all but three. Tom didn't move, and neither did two of the mourners, a teenage girl and a woman who might have been in her late thirties or early forties.

"What you want here, mister?" the older woman asked Tom. Her voice wasn't exactly hostile, but it was far from warm.

"I just came to see them lay Lucas to rest," he said. "I hope he's someplace better now."

"You knew my daddy?" the girl asked him.

"You're Lucas's daughter? Yeah, I knew him for a while."

"I didn't know Lucas had no white friends," the older woman said.

"Well, he had one," Tom said. "For all the good it did him."

The woman eyed him for a few more seconds, then said, "Hey, you're that Tom Dart, ain't you?"

"Yes'm, that's me."

"Lucas wrote about you in a couple of his letters. He said you were one of them guys a man don't hardly know at all, but who are good friends just the same. He thought pretty highly of you."

"Really? That's nice to know. I got lucky and some friends of mine helped me clear my name. You probably heard about it in the news. I just wish Lucas had been able to do the same. He told me about what happened."

"Yeah," the woman said. "He done what they said he done, sure enough, but he had a good reason for it."

"I know he did," Tom said.

"Well," said the woman, "it's nice to meet you, I reckon. My name's Mattie. Mattie Horne. My daughter's name is Felicia."

"It's nice to meet you," Tom said, astonishing the two women by offering to shake their hands. "Lucas told me a lot about the both of you. I wish there was something I could do for you."

"Ain't nothing to be done now," Mattie said with a shrug, gesturing toward the rapidly-filling grave. "It's enough you kept Lucas company when he was in such a bad place. Say, I don't suppose you'd care to come out to our place for dinner, would you? We're just about to go back there, and we've got plenty. Folks been bringing us stuff for two days now."

Tom smiled. "Yeah, I'd like that. Maybe we could discuss some things too."

"Like what things?"

"Well, I mean about what happened, you know. What about the man responsible? The one who attacked your daughter." He nodded toward the girl. "What is his name?"

EPILOGUE

One day in early October, Joe Perrone asked Mirabelle Darcy to accompany him down into the subterranean warren of rooms beneath Tull House.

"I've got a bit of a surprise ready for you," he said.

"What the hell is all this? I've got work to do."

Perrone had been behaving strangely for several weeks. He had been absent from the house for long periods of time, on some business that couldn't have been related to the Bay Phantom. Maybe this had something to do with that.

"It will wait," he said. "I've got someone I want you to see, Mirabelle. You'll have a million questions, I know, and I'll answer all of them, I promise."

He led her into the room he used as an office. There was someone there, standing beside the desk.

It was a man, and Mirabelle knew him. Though he had aged appreciably since the last time she'd seen him, so long ago, his face was unmistakable. Seeing it, and the familiar expression it wore, took her back to her girlhood in a way that made her dizzy.

She looked at Perrone. Gaped at him, actually. The look was a desperate question.

He nodded.

"That can't be," she said, knowing she was wrong, wanting to be wrong, fearing she was right.

"It is," Perrone said. "It's him, I assure you, Mirabelle."

"You've got one hell of a lot of explaining to do," she said, her voice quavering. "And it had better be good. But right now—Oh, who gives a shit?"

She put her hands on either side of Perrone's face, drew him to her, and kissed him firmly on the mouth. Then she ran to her father and threw her arms around him. He hugged her back. Both of them had tears in their eyes.

So did Joe Perrone.

Today was good. Tomorrow would take care of itself.

THE END

ABOUT OUR CREATORS

WRITER –

CHUCK MILLER - was born in Ohio, lived in Alabama for many years, and now resides in Norman, Oklahoma. He is a Libra whose interests include monster movies, comic books, music and writing. He holds a BA in creative writing from the University of South Alabama.

He is the creator/writer of TALES OF THE BLACK CENTIPEDE, THE INCREDIBLE ADVENTURES OF VIONNA VALIS AND MARY JANE KELLY, THE BAY PHANTOM CHRONICLES, and THE MYSTIC FILES OF DOCTOR UNKNOWN JUNIOR. He has also written stories featuring such classic characters as Jill Trent: Science Sleuth, Armless O'Neil, The Griffon, and others.

Miller received the BEST NEW WRITER OF 2011 Award from Pulp Ark. His first novel, the critically acclaimed "Creeping Dawn: The Rise of the Black Centipede" was published in 2011 by Pro Se Press. The second installment in the Black Centipede series, "Blood of the Centipede" was published in 2012. "Black Centipede Confidential" is slated for release in 2013. Also due in 2013 is "Vionna and the Vampires," the first installment of "The Incredible Adventures of Vionna Valis and Mary Jane Kelly."

http://theblackcentipede.blogspot.com/

INTERIOR ILLUSTRATOR –

KEVIN PAUL SHAW BRODEN, - initially seeking a career in comic books, took art courses throughout his education - only to eventually discover that no matter what the media, he was a storyteller at heart. Kevin received a BA in Art (emphasizing Narrative Illustration) from California State University, Fullerton (Fullerton, CA); before that, he worked on the HORNET newspaper as a reporter/illustrator while earning his AA at Fullerton College.

One of Kevin's early jobs teamed him with some of the talent that launched Supreme for Image Comics. You can even find a special "thank you" to Kevin in SUPREME #1. He storyboarded the music video for

BiGod20's "One," as well as videos for John Wesley Harding and Kristin Hersch as part of Summer Arts in Humboldt, CA. Also, he's been contracted to do illustrations for commercials and television series pitches. The textbooks GARDNER'S GUIDE TO WRITING AND PRODUCING ANIMATION and GARDNER'S GUIDE TO PITCHING AND SELLING ANIMATION feature all interior art done by Kevin. With his wife and creative partner, Shannon Muir, Kevin created the online comic FLYING GLORY AND THE HOUNDS OF GLORY, which has been in existence over 15 years. His artwork has also been seen as the interior illustration for Ralph L. Angelo, Jr's "Against Fire and Stone" tale in LEGENDS OF NEW PULP FICTION by Airship 27 Productions, the cover art for the anthology NEWSHOUNDS from Pro Se Press (which also features his story "Stop the Presses!"), and as cover art for self-published e-books he's authored and released which include the REVENGE OF THE MASKED GHOST series and the CLOCKWORK GENIE MYSTERIES.

Oh, and yes, he does have FOUR NAMES. It's a family thing, but it comes in quite handy... FOUR NAMES OF PROFESSIONAL CREATIVITY.

COVER ARTIST –

CHRIS RAWDING – is an eminent artist, educator and outdoor enthusiast. He has been a keen artist from his early days living on the South Shore of Massachusetts where he currently resides with his two sons. After attending the Museum School of Fine Arts and receiving his Bacherlor's in Commercial Illustration from the Art Institute of Boston, he now specializes in digital illustration, caricature design, branding and book illustration, as well as, screen printing and log design. His distinctive comic art style combined with his creativity and passion takes the subject matter to another level and uses color that don't exist in the real world, but makes them believable and turns them into edgy, eye-catching designs. As an eclectic visionary his gallery includes; pop culture, steampunk chic, superheroes and famous phantoms. For the past 20 years, he likes to take rish and pushes his concepts beyond the ordinary with a knack for modern, bold and organic design.

www.rawding.daportfolio.com

WHAT'S GONE BEFORE...

Mobile Alabama in the early 1920s is a hot-house of history, tradition, political corruption and racial bigotry. Amidst this landscape of both grandeur and depravity arises a new avenger to battle the forces of evil and injustice. He is the mysterious Bay Phantom, a dark clad warrior willing to mete out justice with his blazing .45s. But beneath this flamboyant mask is the often inept, naïve Joseph Perrone, heir to a commercial fisheries empire.

Perrone's one amazing asset is his partner, the beautiful Mirabelle Darcy, a young black woman with the ninth highest I.Q. in the world. An engineering genius, it is Mirabelle who provides Perrone with the guidance to see him through the deadly and macabre challenges that await them. A secret Crime Lord is attempting to take over the city and has unleashed a blood-thirsty Werewolf and a bizarre assassin known as the Black Embalmer to carry out his insidious plans.

Now it is up to Mirabelle and the Bay Phantom to save their city with the help of an Austrian doctor named Sigmund Freud. And that's only the beginning!

When a shadowy group of criminals start shaking down restaurants in Mobile, Joe Perrone once again dons the cloak and goggles of the Bay Phantom. Shortly thereafter, wealthy young men begin dropping dead without warning. What do these things have in common with a mysterious psychic, a sinister funeral home, and a nationalist movement known as the Transatlantic Patriots Guild?

That is what the Bay Phantom must learn, and he must do it without his trusted aide, Mirabelle Darcy. She is away on a mission of her own; one that necessitates her breaking into the Leavenworth Federal Penitentiary. Thus left to his own devices, can the Phantom thwart the Cannibal Guild and their deadly assassin, the Mummifier? Or will he become their next victim?

Once again Chuck Miller offers up a thrilling new adventure set in the Deep South and starring his original pulp hero; The Bay Phantom. This is pulp action with an added spicy kick.

www.ingramcontent.com/pod-product-compliance
Lightning Source LLC
Chambersburg PA
CBHW051127260626
47170CB00005B/1699

* 9 7 8 1 9 4 6 1 8 3 8 1 1 *